ISOLDE, LADY DE

THE MORTIMER

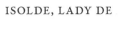

Best Wishes
Fran Norton

ISOLDE, LADY DE AUDLEY: THE MORTIMER MYTH

FRAN NORTON

YOUCAXTON PUBLICATIONS

OXFORD & SHREWSBURY

Other books by this author:
In the Shadow of a Tainted Crown
Throne of Shame
The Twisted Legacy of Maud de Braose

ISBN: 978-1-912419-50-0
Printed and bound in Great Britain.
Published by YouCaxton Publications 2018
YCBN: 01

YouCaxton Publications
enquiries@youcaxton.co.uk

CONTENTS

DRAMATIS PERSONAE

Actual Historical Characters

Edward I King of England
Edward, Prince of Wales Son of Edward I and Queen Eleanor of Castille
Margaret of France Second wife of Edward I
Robert Winchelsea Archbishop of Canterbury
Robert Burnell Bishop of Bath and Wells and Chancellor; friend of Edward I
Isolde de Audley Wife of Sir Hugh de Audley and Walter Balun
Sir Hugh de Audley Second husband of Isolde
Sir Walter Balun First husband of Isolde
Sir Reginald de Balun Brother of Sir Walter Balun and brother-in-law to Isolde
John Balun Nephew of Sir Walter Balun, son of Reginald Balun
Maud de Braose [Lady Mortimer] Widow of Roger Mortimer [d:1282] Lord of Wigmore
Sir Edmund Mortimer, Lord of Wigmore 2nd son of Roger Mortimer and Maud de Braose
Margaret Fiennes Wife of Sir Edmund Mortimer
Roger Mortimer Eldest son of Edmund Mortimer and Margaret Fiennes
Maud [Maudie] FitzAlan[, Lady Burnell] Granddaughter to Maud de Braose and Roger Mortimer
Philip Burnell Husband of Maudie and nephew to Robert Burnell, Chancellor of England
Richard FitzAlan, Earl of Arundel Brother of Maudie and grandson of Roger Mortimer and Maud de Braose

Ela Longespé Widow of James de Audley and mother of Hugh and Nicolas

Nicolas de Audley, Lord of Heleigh Brother-in-law to Isolde

Lady Katherine Giffard Wife of Nicolas de Audley

Thomas de Audley Eldest son of Nicolas and Lady Katherine

Ela de Audley Sister to Thomas and daughter of Nicolas and Katherine

Piers Gaveston Companion and 'favourite' of Prince Edward

Roger Damory Young nobleman who later becomes 'favourite' to Edward II

James de Audley Eldest son of Sir Hugh and Isolde de Audley

Hugh [the younger] Second son of Sir Hugh and Isolde de Audley

Katherine [Kate] de Audley Daughter of Isolde and Hugh de Audley

Alice de Audley Daughter of Isolde and Hugh de Audley

Hugh Despenser [the younger] Eldest son of Sir Hugh Despenser the elder enemy of The Mortimers, later 'favourite' of Edward II

Robert Brus [Bruce] [the younger]Earl of Carrick, later King of Scotland

Robert Brus [the elder] Maudie's 'husband' and father of the King of Scotland

Henry de Lacy, Earl of Lincoln Friend and advisor of Edward I

John de Warenne, Earl of Surrey Friend and advisor of Edward I

Roger Bigod, Earl of Norfolk Wealthy and powerful nobleman

Aymer de Valence, Earl of Pembroke Supporter of Edward I

Thomas Plantagenet, Earl of Lancaster Nephew to King Edward I

Alice de Lacy, Countess of Lancaster Wife of Thomas and daughter of the Earl of Lincoln

Sir William Latimer Nobleman and supporter of Edward I

William Wallace Scottish rebel

John Comyn, Lord of Badenoch 'Red Comyn' contender for the Scottish throne

All the names mentioned in the Scottish wars are actual figures in historical records.

Fictional Characters

Ela Companion to Isolde
Sir Guy de Longeville Lover of Lady Maude de Braose
Brendon Squire to Sir Nicolas de Audley and later to his brother
Miles Squire to Hugh de Audley
Master and Mistress Linus Steward and housekeeper to Isolde
Father Melor Priest to Hugh and Isolde
Master Gregory Physician to Hugh and Isolde
Yancy Head Groom to Hugh and Isolde de Audley
Lady Ankaret Dampierre Mistress to Hugh de Audley
Silas and Sarah Wood Tenants of the de Audleys

PREFACE

In 1272, whilst on a Crusade in the Holy Land, Edward Plantagenet inherited a kingdom that had been fractured by civil war and dissension. Upon his return resentment still festered against his Angevin kinsmen and the memory of his father, Henry III's refusal to uphold the terms of the Magna Carta, had never truly been resolved. Meantime, the long standing wars in Wales still continued.

During his father's ineffectual reign, Edward's ambitions had simmered and aptly demonstrated his true warrior spirit at the Battle of Evesham in 1265, when he had crushed his father's enemy, Simon de Montfort, the Earl of Leicester.

Some believe he had vowed to take the Cross and join Philip, the French King on his Crusade, to atone for his actions during that day. But Henry III had previously vowed to go on Crusade; but with failing health, left his son to fulfill the promise.

Edward had eventually crushed the Welsh resistance building a string of great stone castles across Wales and with the death of the last Welsh Prince Daffyd, at Shrewsbury, turned his attentions to Scotland. The death of King Alexander in 1286, and with the death of his granddaughter the Maid of Norway, left a void in the line of succession. At first Edward acted as mediator his aims however, were not to remain as such but to seize the Scottish crown for himself.

On to this backdrop we meet Isolde [Mortimer], the illegitimate daughter of one of the great Marcher Lords, Sir Roger Mortimer of Wigmore. After his death in 1282, Isolde finds she is to marry a man as old as her father. So let us travel back to medieval England and meet Isolde and follow her stormy life through the final years of the reign of Edward I.

ACKNOWLEDGMENTS

I would like to express my sincere thanks to the following people who have helped over the past two years. First and foremost, to John Fleming, for generously allowing me to use his thesis on Henry [de] Audley. To Barbara Wright, who has gone beyond the 'call of duty' in verifying the medieval court records and sending me copies of some of her work on the Mortimer Cartulary. To Douglas Richardson, whose discovery of the true identity of Isolde after 700 years, is worthy of great praise. My thanks go to Kathryn Warner, Dr. Ian Mortimer and Dr. Paul Dryburgh, for their kind help over the past months.

I would also like to give a special mention to the work of the late Thelma W Lancaster of the Audley History Society and to Fiona Jane Watson, for her work on the Scottish wars. A huge thank you to both Gill McHattie, who has given her precious time to edit this book and Philip Beddows, for his detailed research on the de Verdun family history.

Writing is a lonely occupation but to have such generous people, willing to share their knowledge and research, makes it all worthwhile. Researching the past is fascinating, frustrating, rewarding and time consuming but reaps a very unique reward all of its own and that is, discovering our history and the people who lived, loved, and strove for their ideals and ambitions.

My final thanks, has to go to Stanton Stevens, of Castle Bookshop in Ludlow for his support and friendship over the years.

Fran Norton

BOOK ONE

MARRIAGES

CHAPTER I

Wigmore 1285

'Do stand still Isolde how can I pin the hem if you are fidgeting?'
Isolde Mortimer stood before a long mirror and screwed her
face up at the reflection.

'The colour does not suit me and what does it matter if the
hem is not level?'

'Of course it matters! Besides, Lady Mortimer would be more
than angry if you did not look your best on your wedding day.'
Isolde looked down at the kneeling figure.

'But I do not wish to marry that old, smelly man with his
broken teeth and foul breath.'

'Nevertheless that is what you will do in two weeks from now.'

'Maybe I will run away!'

'And pray where would you go? You have no money or lands
of your own. Do you wish to end up like your poor mama?'
Isolde kicked out and knocked the kneeling woman to the
floor.

'How dare you speak to me thus!' Isolde's voice was icy.

Gasping, the figure rose and caught Isolde tightly by the arm.

'I have loved and looked after your welfare for these past ten
years and this is how you treat me. I hope Sir Walter beats you
regularly and makes your life a misery.' With that, Mistress
Ela walked purposefully to the door and slammed it as she left.

'Oh! My Lady, I fear you have really upset Mistress Ela I have
never seen her so angry.'

Isolde scowled at the young maid. 'It is not your place to
speak without being spoken to and I will not remind you again.'

The girl bowed her head and hurriedly finished putting
away the jewels, which had been out on display for selection

for the forthcoming occasion. Hastily she also left; her cheeks flame red at the brusque chastisement. Isolde Mortimer was known for her sharp tongue and many of the servants resented serving her as they judged her to be no true lady, being the late Lord Mortimer's bastard daughter.

As Isolde was about to leave her chamber the heavy door swung open to reveal the imposing figure of Lady Maud Mortimer, Baroness of Wigmore.

'Exactly what is going on here?'

Isolde stood rooted to the spot as she knew by the expression on the face of her visitor

would be useless to lie. With reluctance she recounted the incident omitting her description of her future husband. 'I will not have you persistently upsetting members of this household. Do you hear me? It will be a relief to one and all when you have moved into your marital home. As you value Mistress Ela so little I see no reason for her to accompany you.'

The words hit Isolde like a physical blow. 'But...........' She had scant time to say more as Maud left without waiting to listen to any further arguments. For some moments Isolde stood still whilst she took in the implications of Lady Mortimer's words. Ela had been her closest companion and friend, almost from the onset of her controversial arrival at Wigmore all those years ago. How could she face living with that odorous old man without the support of Ela? As she stood pondering on her next move she began to realise what Ela had said was true. Where would she go? What alternative was there for a penniless bastard? Besides, when she became Lady Balun she would have a household of her own to run as *she* saw fit. The longer she considered the notion the more it began to appeal to her, the only drawback was the thought of the marriage bed; she gagged at the very idea. But then she smiled to herself, she could plead her age, pretend that she was not yet old enough to become a wife in the physical sense and the idea grew. It would be quite easy to plead that she was too young for at fifteen, she had not developed breasts of any real size and her figure was still immature and girlish. As she took off the fine woollen kirtle and dainty lawn shift, she felt more confident than she had of late. Now she must seek Ela's forgiveness for she did not wish to be parted from the only person she felt any deep affection for.

As Isolde donned her every day kirtle of brown wool, she began to compose her apologies, for she had to change the decisions of both Lady Mortimer and Ela. She knew eventually the latter would succumb and be reconciled but Lady Mortimer was a completely different matter, she would not be so easily gulled. However, Isolde was not about to accept defeat and as she made her way towards Ela's chamber she shrugged her shoulders and changed her expression.

After tapping lightly on the door Isolde entered and looking suitably crestfallen, she went and knelt before the seated figure.

'Oh! Ela, please, please forgive me! I felt so overwrought by the very thought of this marriage.'

The older woman raised her hand.

'I do not wish to hear your excuses, what you did was unforgiveable. You strike out at those who only wish to help you. Over the years I had hoped your shrewish traits would subside but they rise to the surface whenever you are faced with situations you find difficult. Maybe in time I will forgive you, but not right now, so please leave.'

Isolde rose and stood for a moment as looked down at the seated figure. She could see Ela had been weeping and she leaned forward to try and embrace the woman who had been the nearest thing to a mother she had known in years. But Ela pushed her away and turned her face leaving the bemused girl in no doubt that this time her actions would not be so easily overlooked and she would have to live with the consequences.

Isolde left with a feeling of a deep sense of loss. She walked slowly towards her own chamber and went and lay down on the bed and closed her eyes. She realised that she was completely alone and she remembered the same emotions she had felt when she had first arrived at Wigmore. Now she was determined to win back Ela's affections and regain Lady Mortimer's esteem and with those thoughts floating through her head she fell into a fitful slumber.

The following day Isolde went about her normal daily routine in a subdued frame of mind. She heard Mass at seven and after breaking her fast she went up to the old nursery where she knew she would find Carys. Sure enough, Carys was ordering the young maids to clean and sort out the chests and cupboards in readiness for when Lord Edmund married and brought his new bride back to Wigmore later that year.

'Ah! Mistress Isolde! What mischief have you been about now?'

'How do you know I have been into any mischief?'

Carys stopped what she was doing, and smiled wryly at the defiant reply.

'Because you - are invariably in some sort of trouble or other!'

Isolde bit back the tart response she was about to utter and remembered she had come here for advice and not to add to the list of her woes. She went and dropped down onto one of the beds and recounted the previous day's events. Carys went and sat on the bed opposite and looked hard at Isolde.

'I thought Ela was upset last night but she would not tell me the reason. Well, this time I do believe you have stepped beyond the boundaries and knowing the two ladies in question, I fear you may have to face up to the outcome of your actions.' Carys continued to study Isolde.

'You have no idea of the pain you have caused Mistress Ela, not to say the annoyance of her ladyship. When will you learn that you cannot abuse people without dire consequences? You will inevitably meet someone one day who will resort to physical violence against you, then how will you feel?' She paused for a moment: 'you have no notion of how many times Mistress Ela has pleaded on your behalf against punishment; has defended you almost daily through the years against one and all. How betrayed she must now feel. You should be ashamed of yourself Miss Isolde. It is also a fact that Lady Mortimer could have sent you into obscurity and forgotten you ever existed but instead she ensured you had a good education and wanted for naught. Again, she must feel thoroughly let down by such peevish behaviour.'

Isolde looked defiantly at the speaker but slowly as the words began to sink in her expression changed to one of shame.

'It has not been easy for me to accept the status of my birth; half noble, half peasant the battles that rage within me do not make for easy living.'

'I know my child, but you have never made life easy for
yourself; always on the defensive, always ready to challenge
and refusing the proffered hand of help.'

Isolde paused.'I never realised how Mistress Ela has tried
to protect me over the years.'

'That lady is a rare unselfish being who should be cherished
not abused. You have no understanding of her trials and
tribulations; you view the world through eyes, which sees
only what affects you personally. You have yet to appreciate
the qualities of others and look only for their defects. You
frequently invite trouble where there should be none, simply
by your attitude.'

Carys moved across the room and took the girl's hands in
hers.

'You have the spirit and the attributes to become a lady of
worth but first you must conquer yourself. Love yourself, then
and only then, can you love others. I learned that lesson decades
ago when I was so brutally wounded and hated myself for what
others had done to me, but eventually, I came to understand
the most important lesson of all that first, I must learn to
live in peace with myself and once I grasped that concept, life
became more bearable. I will speak to Mistress Ela on your
behalf but only if I have your word you will strive to be worthy
of her forgiveness and try to make amends in the future.'

Isolde lowered her eyes for an instant before replying; 'thank
you Carys, I will be indebted to you for that. I cannot promise
I can change overnight but I will consider your words carefully
and try and repair my relationship with Ela – if she will let me.'

Carys bent down and whispered. 'As Lady Balun you will
have a chance at a new life where you are mistress and if
you are as smart as I think you are, then you will wrap your
husband around your little finger and gain control over your
own destiny.'

Isolde grinned up at the ravaged face and squeezed her hands.

'I had begun to think along those lines and besides, I could
plead I was still too young to bed – at least for a few months,
by which time I could have the old man eating out of my hand.'

'You would have to guard your tongue and temper and
develop a girlish side and play the coquette.'

Isolde giggled. 'You mean play a part like a mummer and hide behind a mask.'

'Well, my advice was not meant for you to become deceitful but to find yourself and grow into a true lady and make all those that have doubted your abilities, eat their words.'

'Do you really believe I can do that?'

'Of course I do, and so do Mistress Ela and Lady Mortimer.'

'I can scarcely credit that her ladyship holds that belief.'

'Ah! That is where you are wrong she knows you have the capability but have until now chosen to ignore it and I am confident she has done the best she can for you in arranging this marriage. I know you do not believe me but she could have easily made a much less prestigious match could she not? Sir Walter is a well respected knight and has proved his worth over the years.'

'I suppose you are right. So, what you are saying is that it is not due to Lord Edmund's imminent marriage that I am to be married off to this aged knight in order to get me away from Wigmore before the new Lady Mortimer arrives.'

Carys chuckled. 'Well I cannot deny I'm certain there is probably more than a grain of truth in that no doubt, but nevertheless, to become Lady Balun is nothing to be ashamed of is it?'

The girl nodded. 'No, I suppose not! I had not even considered being a full blown Lady before.'

'So now all we have to do is repair your relationship with Mistress Ela.'

'Do you think that is possible? She did seem so cold when I tried yesterday.'

'Give it time and I will apprise you of the outcome of my intercedence. Now I must get on as these days my energies are much reduced and I have to take a nap after noon.'

Isolde rose and kissed Carys on her scarred cheek.

'No doubt you are right but I have never felt I belong with these Mortimers and nothing can change that, however, I will remember your words of advice. My only fear is that I have lost the love of the one person whose love I need the most.'

'Do not despair child, love has a great capacity for forgiveness and Mistress Ela is not given to holding grudges but I think it will be up to you to prove your resolve to change your attitude to others? Now be off with you.'

Isolde Mortimer left the familiar surroundings of the nursery and made her way back to her own chamber. Carys was right, it did depend on her to make her own life better and as she sat brushing her thick, black hair, she finally faced the fact that she had hated herself all these years and that had been at the root of her spite but knowing the cause could not alter her own perception of herself instantly. As she continued with her task, she stared hard at the face in the reflector. The image she saw staring back was not of a pretty damsel but neither was it plain. The oval face had a pale, clear complexion with high cheekbones and a mass of black curling hair. The dark eyes were wary and almond shaped, her nose was straight but too narrow to be attractive and the lips although well defined, she judged too thin to be inviting. She flung the brush away from her dissatisfied with what she saw but then she began to pull faces at herself and mimicked a smile then tilted her head this way and that viewing herself from every conceivable angle. She leant forward and cupped her face in her hands and adopted the pose of a coquette then pretended to play the part of a noble Lady and slowly saw that instead of a waspish countenance she could appear almost attractive. Isolde resolved to practice these new looks and begin to play the part, not of the cuckoo, as she had always felt herself to be, but of a true member of the Mortimer family. As she turned back, she dropped a deep and graceful curtsy for, if Isolde failed at many social graces, she excelled at dancing and music and as she danced around her chamber, she was determined to strive to become a noblewoman in truth.

CHAPTER II

Edmund Mortimer sat watching his mother as she read the list of guests who would be attending the forthcoming marriage of his half sister, Isolde.

'Balun appears content with the wench's marriage portion. At least Wigmore will be quit of her awkward presence once and for all.'

'Indeed! I shall be more than happy to see the back of that little shrew. She has always had an unsettling affect on those around her.' She looked up and smiled at her favourite son.

'Once I have packed up and left for Radnor then Wigmore will be ready to welcome its new mistress, Lady Margaret.'

'If she fulfils her duties with half as much success as you have done Mama, then I shall feel well satisfied. Are you sure I cannot persuade you to stay and help her settle in?'

'I know it may be traditional for a young bride to live with the family she will marry into but circumstances have not been conducive in your case and I feel that she would find my presence somewhat ....difficult. I am not oblivious to my forceful reputation, therefore, I feel that my decision to remove myself to Radnor will not only please her but suit me also. I have served my time as matriarch to the Mortimer family. I am happy to step aside for a younger generation to take the reins and content in the knowledge that its future successes lies in the capable hands of my son. I look forward to my time at Radnor for it has always been a favourite place for me.'

'With Lord de Longeville?' Edmund watched his mother's face as he posed the question.

'Guy has accepted the command of the Castle, a necessary position as there is still unrest in the area. Besides, I know you trust my judgement and I find having a friend in charge of the troops most comforting.'

'Friend!' Edmund chuckled. 'You may fool many Mama but Guy de Longeville is far more to you than a friend, is he not?'

Maud's expression had not altered.

'What are you accusing your mother of, having a lover?

'Not accusing, merely stating what I see when you are in each other's company. You appear at ease and share so many views on important matters. Pray do not think I am judging you Mama, in fact. I am glad that de Longeville will be at Radnor to look after you, for he has proved his worth both, as a knight of distinction and an able negotiator and diplomat. We are lucky he has chosen to return to England where such talents can be used to good effect by the esteemed Lady Mortimer.'

'Then we are both satisfied with the arrangement.' Maud smiled artlessly as she spoke.

'Now, what do you think of Balun entering his name for the tournament?'

'He obviously wishes to impress his young bride. Methinks he carries too much weight these days to pose a dashing figure in the saddle. I shall be interested to see the size of his charger.' Maud smiled broadly at the thought.

'Well, he will be easily spotted in the mêlée, of that there is no doubt.'

'I do not wish for such a show of arms upon my marriage; I would like the event to be more in keeping with my bride's character, dignified and stately. I have spent too many days in the saddle these past few years so it will be good to take time to enjoy more relaxing pursuits for *my* wedding than those chosen by Sir Walter.'

'Have you given any thought to the members of my household you wish to stay at Wigmore?'

Edmund nodded. 'Arthur, I feel would be an indispensable asset, as he is familiar with all the accounting procedures and has a valuable network of agents and merchants. I would also like to keep Carys but will allow her the choice to either, leave with you or stay and help my wife as she has done for you over the years.'

'Of course, but Errol I insist remain with me, so too, Hal and young Gyles. Rufus has decided to retire and live here at Wigmore. I know your father left him well provided for but I feel he will need to know he is still valued, so hope you can find time to visit him.'

Edmund looked at his mother.

'As always your suggestions are admirable; as the former have served you for so long and nowadays I have my own loyal body of servants, believe that is an excellent solution.'

'Now tell me if the rumours are true that the king is taking steps to reduce the power of the church here in England?'

Edmund sighed.

'Did you really believe that Edward Plantagenet would not make the church feel his displeasure at repeatedly refusing to allow his friend and Chancellor, Robert Burnell, the See of Canterbury? He has no jurisdiction in ecclesiastical rulings from Rome however, secular issues are another matter and I believe he is exploring where he can legally curtail their powers.'

'Edward never lets a slight go unpunished or a service unrewarded.'

'Unlike his father, Edward has a close knit core of friends and advisors whom he listens to and although they may disagree on occasions, he accepts that they speak only out of their personal beliefs and not to cause mischief.'

'There is no denying, he and Burnell are bringing stability to the governance of the country, maybe not to everyone's immediate benefit but by stamping the king's authority in every quarter it gives men the belief that their voices are finally being heard and their complaints addressed.'

Edmund nodded and added, 'at least he has crushed the Welsh, although there are still pockets of resistance and will be for the foreseeable future, I fear.'

'Well, I am proud of the part my sons played in bringing about the downfall of Llywelyn ap Gruffydd, although the enmity between England and Wales is still burning and has a long and festering history of grievances which will take generations to wane. War is never good for the people. They have to bear the extra taxation, which, in turn causes hardships brought about by disruption not only to their income, but also, to their whole way of life especially if the men-folk are called upon to take arms or die in the service of their country.'

Maud waved her hand in a circular motion.

'We have experienced such disruptions here at Wigmore and also know it has affected every noble house in the land. But at least with Edward, I feel confident that he has a vision of how he sees the future for his kingdom, even though the initial period may prove difficult; in the long term I believe it will be for the betterment of all.'

'Amen to that! No doubt, the churchmen will pose another challenge when the new restrictions begin to bite. I know from firsthand experience that any challenge to a Bishop's authority is met with fierce opposition and is usually crushed but, against the will of Edward of England – well, that may prove to be another matter entirely!'

'Then it will be interesting to see where Burnell stands on the matter, with Rome, or the king or neither.'

Edmund looked thoughtful for a moment.

'I do not believe he is another Thomas a Beckett. Burnell is a man who will serve his own conscience, in that I am certain, and will somehow bring about a solution which will be acceptable to both sides. He is an able and charming man with a natural gift of diplomacy, frequently resolving difficult situations, almost seamlessly. He understands both Edward and the power of Rome, and therefore, although it may be a bumpy road, in my opinion, he is the right man to reconcile the two parties, maybe not immediately but at some point in the future.'

'Well we have weathered far worse storms and know there will be many more to face in the coming years. The wind of change that is blowing throughout the land will bring about some disasters, but as long as we can ride the storm and remain loyal to the king, I feel the fortunes of the Mortimers' will survive.'

'The future holds no fears for you, my dearest Mama?'

'Of course it does, but it is my experience to face the trials of each day as they arise and not anticipate an outcome. All too often, Fate has a nasty way of changing the rules when we least expect them!'

'There speaks a pragmatic woman.'

'Well enough chit chat, I am sure you have more important matters to attend to than waste time on an old woman.'

Edmund Mortimer threw back his head and laughed out loud.

'Talking to you is, and never has been a waste of time, and you well know that fact.'

Maud's face split into a cheeky grin.

'I am merely testing *your* diplomacy, for 'tis my belief, a lot more may be gained by talking than fighting.'

'Indeed!'

'Returning to more pertinent matters, I am pleased Isolde's wedding is to be at St. Bartholomew's in Much Marcle rather than here at Wigmore, it gives me more time to prepare for your wedding occasion. Just think, in a few days time our little minx will become Lady Balun.'

Edmund rose, went and kissed his mother's brow, and left giving a big wink as he departed. Maud remained seated for a moment as she mused on how life was about to take her on another step of her journey and she felt a sense of satisfaction at the prospect. Soon she would no longer be responsible for Isolde's welfare; Edmund was about to make a prestigious match with the Queen's kinswoman, the Lady Margaret Fiennes, leaving her free to return to Radnor and live with her beloved Guy de Longeville. She crossed herself and offered up a prayer of thanks. Finally, with a clear conscience she could flout convention but – discreetly. She did not wish to involve her family name with any untoward scandal. As she rose to leave, she smiled to herself; soon, she could shake the dust of Wigmore from her shoes and leave to enjoy the remainder of her years where she chose. The prospect pleased her deeply.

If Maud faced the future with optimism and hope, it was not so for Isolde Mortimer and even the thought of becoming a Lady could not quell her doubts and fears. Sir Walter Balun was a respected knight but he was too advanced in years to be her husband of choice. In fact, he was older than her late father would have been had he lived. She wrestled with her emotions knowing that if she remained at Wigmore she would soon come under the jurisdiction of Edmund's wife, Lady Margaret

Fiennes and by all accounts, she was a pious, learned and handsome young woman. What would they have in common – nothing! Did she really want to live under such a regime? Isolde's unsettled thoughts did not make the forthcoming marriage any more appealing even though her wedding attire was of the very highest quality and she knew most girls would be envious of such finery.

Although Isolde acknowledged that Ela had worked tirelessly to ensure all the garments for the ceremony were finished, there were still many of the trivial details to complete, for example, would there be enough spring flowers to fill the church, and the dyes on her patens - would they dry to the require shade in time? Then there was her headdress still to choose, and knowing which one would suit her best? She could no longer turn to Ela for advice and Isolde admitted to herself exactly how much she missed their former relationship. However, there was one person who would tell her the truth and that was Lady Mortimer and with that thought Isolde made her way to the apartments of the Lady who still ruled Wigmore.

Lady Maud Mortimer heard the knock on her door and indicated to the page to open it. When she saw who the visitor was she dismissed her attendants for she did not wish anyone to hear Isolde complaints; if word reached the ears of Sir Walter, then it may prove detrimental to the girl's future relationship with her husband.

'Pray what brings you here today?' Maud looked enquiringly at Isolde.

'I seek your advice, my Lady.'

'And how may I help you?' Maud noted the unusual uncertainty in the speaker for Isolde invariably appeared to be on the offensive and was rarely known to seek anyone's advice.

'I have to pick a headdress for the occasion and........'

'Surely Mistress Ela is on hand for such matters?'

'She says she is too busy with finishing the stitching on my robes.'

'I see no reason for any a headdress, young brides have their hair dressed in a flattering style adorned with either flowers or jewels, sometimes a simple circlet of gold or silver but only after their wedding begin to wear a headdress.

'Oh! I thought ....'

'Well – has that answered your question?'

Isolde nodded and turned on her heel and upon reaching the doorway looked back and made a brief gesture of thanks. As she ran down the passageway, she felt that her question had somehow, made her look foolish, and upon entering her own chamber, she slammed the door, and went and lay on her bed her face flushed red with a mixture of anger and embarrassment. The sooner she became Lady Balun the better, and later when she rose, she no longer felt at odds with herself and vowed to ensure that she would look her very best on the day she became a bride.

§

The day of Isolde's wedding finally arrived with all thoughts of the discomforts of the journey now forgotten, as the church of Saint Bartholomew began to fill with the colourful congregation. There were loud murmurings as the dignitaries took their places. An hour later, Lady Mortimer watched the young bride intently as she walked slowly down the aisle and felt more than satisfied at what she saw. Isolde looked resplendent in her rich kirtle of deep cream wool, over which was a fine silk tunic of palest blue decorated with hand stitched cornflowers with wild roses of pink and white depicted trailing down the front and around the hem. The girl's thick mane of hair had been tamed and braided with ribbons and pearl droplets had been threaded through the heavy braids. She moved slowly by Maud with great dignity and the Lady of Wigmore felt a great sense of satisfaction. Maybe the occasion had finally wrought the longed for change in Isolde as she realised what all her years of training had been about. Inwardly, Maud felt relief, for Isolde was ever an unpredictable character and the whole ceremony could have proved a catastrophe.

During the solemn service, Maud looked up at her son Edmund and smiled as he took his place beside her, after carrying out his part of the ceremony by giving away the bride. Sir Walter Balun looked as though he would burst with pride as he gazed down at his bride. Throughout the ceremony Isolde's hands shook, as the heavy gold band was being placed on her finger. Sir Walter had to hold tight, to her hand to steady her uncontrollable trembling.

The couple walked back down the aisle together as man and wife and Lady Mortimer breathed a long sigh of relief. What happened next would be out of her hands but at least she had done her duty and ensured that her late husband's daughter had made a worthy match. In the Great Hall the newly married couple greeted their guests as they filed passed, receiving all the wishes for health and good fortune.

The evening festivities proved raucous and loud. Isolde sat bolt upright, her dark eyes watching the Marcher lords and their wives and daughters as they made merry. She did not miss the expressions of the men and women or some of the lewd remarks aimed at her husband, accompanied by knowing winks and gestures. She encouraged Sir Walter to drink freely throughout the night and watched as his face became redder and more mottled with each passing hour. When the time came for the bedding ritual, Isolde begged her husband to stay for just one more dance and one more toast but eventually she ran out of excuses and made her way to their bedchamber. Feeling embarrassed, Isolde felt helpless, whilst she was undressed for the time honoured ritual.

Once out of her rich wedding garments the fine lawn nightshift was pulled down over her pale shoulders. The pearls and ribbons, she had worn in her hair, were roughly snatched out by unfamiliar hands. Ela was unable to attend the new Lady Balun for the mischievous pranksters had locked her in her room.

In the darkness, Isolde lay waiting for her husband. She knew he would be accompanied by his band of friends and she offered up a prayer that he would be too drunk to indulge in the expected marital act. She heard the laughing voices, full of innuendoes and ribaldry and shivered. Finally, Sir Walter managed to get rid of his attendants by warning them if they persisted in remaining in the bedchamber he would never be able to perform his husbandly duties. As the sound of the noisy crowd began to diminish, Sir Walter reached over and touched Isolde's shoulder.

'I fear I have drunk too much wine,' he hesitated before continuing, 'have no fear child, I will ask nothing of you tonight.'

Isolde turned over to look up at the huge figure sat perched on the edge of the bed.

'I want you to know I will cherish and look to your wellbeing for the rest of my life. I am well aware I am not a young girl's idea of a Sir Lancelot but even though I do not look the part well – I can at least act the gallant.'

There had been no hint of slurring in his speech and the girl heard the sincerity in his words. He rose and left the bemused bride lying alone in the dark to return to his own chamber. Slowly, the tension eased from Isolde's body and eventually she slept. The following morning she found the distraught Ela busily laying out the clothes for the day's tournament.

'You should know I was locked in my chamber last night so, if you thought I left you unattended of my free will then, please think again Mistress.'

'Oh, Ela, yesterday was filled with so many extraordinary things, I guessed some mischief must have overtaken you.' She smiled wistfully then whispered.

'I am still a virgin!'

Ela's expression of surprise amused Isolde and she chuckled as she recounted the previous evening's scene.

'Well all I can say is my regard for Sir Walter has risen tenfold. He proved true to his knightly vows and I am happy that you have found such a husband. Obviously, age has served him and you well in this instance, has it not?'

'Mmm but, what we must not do is betray his chivalry on this occasion, for I would not have him made fun of! If he has shown regard for me then I will do likewise.'

Ela nodded. This boded well for her young protégé. The aged knight had, by this single act of consideration, proved himself in the eyes of his young bride, a good start to any marriage but especially to this one. How long Isolde's present mood would last Ela could not be certain, for she was renowned for her mercurial temperament but at least it would make today's event more enjoyable.

At noon, the herald entered the arena and read out a long list of names of the participants of the tournament, followed by the loud clarion to alert the knights and squires to take their places for the mêlée to begin. Wagers were placed, banners waved and the voices of supporters rose as the first line of combatants clashed. The squeals of the horses mingled with the shouts and groans as the fight proceeded in earnest.

Isolde strained her eyes to catch a sight of her husband's great charger and spied him in the thick of the fighting. For what seemed like an age, the wave of knights charged, retreated, and charged again; individual battles had begun to emerge and the voices of the spectators joined in the general cacophony of noise. It was during a charge when Sir Walter's mighty horse, Goliath, stumbled and appeared to have been wounded, for it suddenly screamed in agony, half reared then turned sharply, dislodging Sir Walter from the saddle. The charger careered away from the fighting and the sickening scene which ensued, caused Isolde and many others to gasp, for Sir Walter's foot had become caught in the stirrup and he was now being dragged away by the stricken horse.

Immediately the herald directed the mounted grooms and squires, who were sat at the side of the arena, to go to Sir Walter's aid. The majority of the combatants continued with the event until eventually the continuous blast of the herald brought the field to a standstill as the battered body of Sir Walter Balun was born on a litter to the surgeon's tent. The wounded charger was led away to his stable to be treated by his groom.

Isolde rose and hurriedly made her way to where her husband lay. At first she was barred from entering and only when the squire realised her identity did he bow and stand aside for her to enter.

'This is no place for you, Lady Balun.' The surgeon's voice was low as he looked up briefly to speak to his patient's young wife.

'Where else should I be pray?'

Isolde moved to where the prone figure lay moaning in agony and knelt beside the battered body of her husband. Blood oozed from many wounds but when she saw the blood trickling from his mouth and ears, Isolde caught her breath and wept silently. She looked at his ashen cheeks and then up to the surgeon who was busily bathing the fallen knight's forehead.

'Will he live?' Isolde's voice was fearful.

'I am afraid he has numerous injuries my Lady, but I would be obliged if you would leave and allow my team to assess the extent of his wounds and treat him without hindrance.'

Isolde nodded, rose and left accompanied by Ela. As they made the way back to the fortified manor house, they were joined by Lady Mortimer.

'How bad are his injuries?'

Isolde looked up at the speaker but appeared as though she had emerged from a dream.

'He is sorely wounded and there is blood streaming from his nose and ears and so many other places, I have never seen such a terrible sight.' She paused. 'He looked ghastly; I could tell the surgeon fears for his life.'

Lady Maud Mortimer spoke sternly but softly.

'Remember, you are now Lady Balun and as such will need to keep control of your own emotions and take charge of your household. There were other combatants that have been injured and therefore will remain until they are fit enough to leave; see that the servants look after all of your remaining guests and let them know how Sir Walter fares. I suspect many have been in his service for a number of years and are fearful he may die. Isolde, you are their mistress now and it is to you that they must receive instruction. I believe your brother-in-law, Sir Reginald, is in attendance and may well try and take charge.' Maud looked intently at the pale face of Isolde, 'now is the time to take the lead but, do it with quiet authority and in a non-confrontational manner, it is your actions now that will be judged in the future, get it right and you will gain respect not resentment. If you wish me to stay, then I will. However, if you want to take charge on your own I will leave on the morrow but will leave Mistress Ela here to help you.'

'I wish you to stay! My wits feel numb but my heart is breaking and I fear I may act rashly at such a time and your advice will be most welcome.'

Although surprised, Maud Mortimer, Lady of Wigmore nodded, gratified that Isolde was seeking help; it would be ironic if the girl was both a bride and a widow within a week. Maud understood how this unique situation could unnerve even the most experienced woman, never mind a girl of barely fifteen.

The older woman reached out and took Isolde's hands, 'you have the courage. Now go and change into more suitable attire and send for the steward.'

Isolde nodded and followed Ela back to her apartments where she duly changed into a dark kirtle.

'Tell the page to bring Master Linus to me!'

Ela did as she was asked and within a short space of time the man who had served Sir Walter for over twenty years, stood before his new mistress. Every line on his face etched in sadness.

'This is not the outcome that was envisaged for this day, Master Linus, but we have to deal with the consequences as Sir Walter would have wished!'

Isolde's words were spoken in little more than a whisper.

'Indeed my Lady!'

'Nevertheless, we will endeavour to carry on and look to the welfare of our guests; in you I rely.'

'Have no fear I will see all is as it should be my lady!'

'I know you will take charge of the servants at this time and I will keep you informed of Sir Walter's condition. I believe his brother believes it is his place to oversee the household – please remind everyone they take their orders from me until Sir Walter can resume his position as head of this household.'

The man bowed then said gravely: 'you will have my full support, Lady Balun.'

Isolde nodded. 'Thank you, Master Linus, I'm afraid I may have to lean on you rather heavily through this stressful time but together, we will uphold the high standards of my stricken husband.'

After his departure Ela looked across at Isolde. 'That was well done!'

'Do you think so? I know I will make mistakes but I mean to try and rise to the challenge as Lady Mortimer has rightly stated – it is how I deal with the coming days I shall be judged and therefore I do not wish to be found wanting. Now let us return and see if there has been any change in my husband's condition.'

CHAPTER III

A week passed during which Sir Walter Balun hung in a world
between the living and the dead. Isolde visited him three times
a day and clung to the hope that he would win his battle to
live but even though his colour had changed from the grey
ashen mask, it was still a deathly white. His breathing was no
longer laboured as he lay in a deep coma.

'Is there still no improvement?'

'I fear not my lady, I will send for you directly if aught
changes. I take this as a sign that every day he survives gives
him a better chance. However, it is my experience that injuries
such as the ones sustained by your husband may have a lasting
effect; he will no longer be the man he once was!'

'You mean – he may be crippled?'

'Yes, or he may not be able to speak, he suffered great trauma
to his head. I cannot tell until he wakes what lasting damage
has been done.'

Isolde nodded. 'I thank you for all of your efforts; whatever
the outcome, it is not for lack of your skills and care but now
is in God's hands.'

The surgeon made the sign of the cross. 'Amen to that!'

Another two days passed, then at ten in the morning, Sir
Walter Balun opened his eyes, sat up and shouted a garbled
phrase and dropped back on his pillows stone dead. Isolde was
now a widow and about to face the ambitions of her brother-in-
law as he quickly moved to seize control of his brother's estates.

If Reginald Balun believed his young sister-in-law was about
to meekly stand by and watch him take charge, he was badly
mistaken. The matter came to a head when a breathless groom
ran to report that Sir Walter's favourite horses, hounds and
falcons were about to be taken away. Isolde sent a page to

summon her steward and gave him the order to put a stop to
the exodus.

Sir Reginald Balun swept into Isolde's chamber his face
red with anger.

'I will not have my orders countermanded by you madam.
I am my brother's executor and know he intended me to
have........'

Isolde raised her hand. 'My lord, obviously you are unaware
that my husband made a new will only weeks before our
marriage and many of his former bequests, were rescinded.'

The look that crossed Sir Reginald's face was of utter
consternation and confusion.

'Why was I not informed of these changes?' his voice shook
with emotion.

'I believe you were away in Wales at the time; no doubt Sir
Walter thought there was time enough to acquaint you with
the changes, Fate however, had other plans.'

'This is unconscionable I need to read this new will with
my own eyes.'

Isolde nodded. 'I have sent for my kinsman who witnessed
the document he will be here within the day. Until such time, I
suggest you instruct your servants to return all of my husband's
livestock back to their proper place.' Without another word
Isolde walked to the door and held it ajar. 'Next time you wish
to speak with me, pray knock before entering.'

He glared down into the pale face of the young widow
muttered some obscenities then turned on his heel and left.
Isolde let out a long sigh of relief. Ela moved towards the
shaking figure.

'You left him in no doubt that you are a true Mortimer and I
feel he will take more care when dealing with you in the future.'

'Surely his own wit should tell him that a wife takes
precedence and even though ours was such a short marriage,
nevertheless, it merely follows the usual pattern of the law.'

'I believe Sir Reginald thought you little more than a girl
and would show no resistance to his authority.'

A slow smile crept over Isolde's sharp features.

'He had not realised, that in such matters, I am my father's
daughter!'

As Isolde had forecast Lord Edmund Mortimer arrived before nightfall and sought a meeting with the irate knight. After a long discussion the two men emerged and it was plain they had arrived at an amicable agreement. Isolde would remain in residence during six months of mourning after which she would move to a comfortable manor house some five leagues away taking the servants who wished to stay in her service, together with all the goods and chattels listed in Sir Walter's will. The dower lands would be in Isolde's ownership for her lifetime together with a tenth of the Balun lands and estates, as laid down in the Magna Carta.

On the day of the funeral Isolde walked between Sir Reginald Balun and Lord Edmund Mortimer to pay their final respects to a man who had been both popular and respected by all who knew him; many genuine tears of grief were shed that day and no one could doubt that his young wife was among their number.

The Great Hall, filled with mourners, left Isolde feeling overwhelmed by their numbers; at the far side of the Hall Lady Mortimer watched the girl who had been the cause of so much disruption to her life in the past few years and noted her discomfort. With consummate ease, Maud made her way to the young widow's side.

'I sense this throng fills you with unease?'

Isolde started. 'I had hoped no one noticed.' Her voice was low and halting.

'To all but those who know you, I believe you have succeeded, however, to those that have known you longer will sense your unease. It is to be expected; you have born a great loss and uncertainty during the past month with noticeable dignity and I commend you. Now you understand why all the lessons you were made to endure over the years are now coming into play and I hope you can see why I was ever insistent that you were never allowed to play truant.'

Isolde looked into the green-grey eyes of the older woman and held her gaze for a long moment.

She still felt the old resentment well up but spoke in even tones. 'I have come to appreciate many of the lessons I learnt at Wigmore over the past years but the one that stands out is not what I learned in any classroom - but the ones I learnt watching you. I must admit I have come to appreciate the strength of your self reliance and have tried, over the past weeks to model myself upon you and how I believed you would deal with such a situation. For that alone, I am deeply indebted to you, Lady Mortimer.'

'There is no debt. I gave your father a promise on his deathbed to look after your welfare for as long as I lived - my promises are not given lightly.'

Without giving Isolde a chance to reply, Lady Mortimer turned and walked back to where her son stood talking to Sir Philip Burnell.

'Ah! Sir Philip there is a matter I would speak with on with regard to my granddaughter.'

The portly figure with his round face and heavy features looked disdainfully at the speaker.

Maud noted how his expression altered and a guarded expression crept across his flushed features.

'I believe Lady Balun would benefit greatly in her time of grief, from a visit from your wife.'

'No doubt that may be, but my wife's place is at my side as is her duty, like all wives.'

'Do I take that to be a refusal my lord?'

Lady Mortimer's voice, although not raised, was clear enough to be heard by those closest to them, the tension quickly spreading around the Hall and the scene attracted much curiosity much to the chagrin of Sir Philip Burnell. Aware he was at the centre of attention his face flushed and he spluttered as he tried to exonerate himself.

'Err! Grief is usually best kept private and suffered in silence.'

'But for one so young and under such unusual circumstances I felt certain you would understand my .... suggestion!'

Edmund Mortimer stepped forward he had seen the look in his mother's eyes and knew she was not about to let this matter go and he did not want to see the issue get out of hand.

'I am sure you have times that your duties take you from home, surely on this occasion you could combine any outstanding commitments whilst Maudie spends time with her kinswoman and thus both matters would be addressed.'

Sir Philip Burnell glanced nervously round at the onlookers and realised he had been out manoeuvred by Lady Mortimer; therefore to try to save face, he nodded but his face had gone a purplish red in his fury.

Edmund Mortimer smiled. 'There, that is settled then, after my wedding ceremony Sir Philip will fulfil his business duties and Maudie can ride over to visit Isolde.'

But, he did not miss the brief look of triumph that flickered across his mother's face.

CHAPTER IV

A few weeks later Lady Maud Burnell rode towards the fortified manor house of her kinswoman, Isolde Balun. Maud had ridden in silence for most of the journey but could not ignore the sense of relief she had felt which had grown, the further she had ridden from Wigmore. Not that she was happy to leave her relatives but that she would be free from the constant watchful eyes of her husband. Marriage had been a complete disappointment for Maud. Her husband possessed none of the charm, dignity and wit of his uncle, Robert Burnell, England's Chancellor. However, his greatest fault was his duplicity; the face he used in public bore no resemblance to the one he wore in private. Only two of the household servants had served him for more than two years and they were in the pay of his father. He had dismissed two of her waiting women for trivial excuses. He ruled by fear and uncertainty, dictating every tiny detail of the household routine. His personal excesses she detested; he over ate, over drank, gambled too heavily and was prone to using his fists when angry. Since her marriage, she had changed from the bright, outgoing girl to a reserved young woman. Her pregnancy had saved her from months of his displeasure but when she had given birth to a daughter instead of the longed for son and heir, there had been a subtle change towards her. However, she was barely seventeen and he assured her there would be plenty of time to give him many sons. The thought made her flesh crawl; she hated any physical contact with him but accepted it was part of her duty.

As the little company turned into the driveway, Maud urged her palfrey forward as she spied the familiar figures of Isolde and Ela standing at the entrance. She dismounted and ran towards them hugging Isolde and then turning to Ela with a big smile of relief etched across her face.

'I am so happy to see you both again and without ....' She did not need to say anything more, they both understood her meaning.

'This is Milly, my maid, who has only been with me for a month, is that not so Milly?'

The young woman dropped a neat curtsey as she nodded.

'There are refreshments waiting and I have put you in the chamber next to mine.' Isolde whispered, as she reached for Maud's hand and they entered the house together; a rare show of affection from Isolde.

The visit had been eagerly anticipated by both Isolde and Ela, not only at the thought of renewing their former relationship after two and a half years but also to glean the details of Edmund's wedding. Between nibbling some of the tasty delicacies and sipping the rich, sweet mead, Maud began to describe the young bride, her clothes and the ceremony which had taken place just days ago.

'And do you think the Lady Margaret a suitable bride for Edmund?' Isolde's question was said without rancour but she was quick to note the wary glance Maud made towards her maidservant. Isolde, understood the warning and promptly answered herself. 'Well, we know she is suitable but do they seem amicable together?'

'I think they looked very happy with each other and we felt somewhat amused to see Uncle Edmund so smitten.'

Maud continued to describe the expensive clothes and furs worn by the guests and the exquisite jewellery adorning the bride; then she began to whirl round the chamber as she exclaimed:

'The musicians were sent by the king, to serenade the bride and groom and I know you would have enjoyed many of their new ballads and melodies. Come Milly, we can show the steps and I will attempt to hum the tunes and knowing your musical ear Isolde, I am certain you will quickly pick up both the music and the dance'.

In an exaggerated gesture, Maud held out her hand to Milly to join her on the floor. At first, the young woman hesitated but then without a word rose and moved to take her place for the demonstration. After a few false starts and many giggles, Maud and her maid eventually succeeded to their satisfaction. Isolde had joined in after a while accompanying the pair on her lute. Ela clapped her hands as the breathless couple left the floor and returned to their seat.

'Milly! Will you fetch my shawl after such exertions I am certain to feel the cold presently.'

Without a word, the maid obediently left.

Maud waited until the girl's footsteps could no longer be heard, before whispering, 'Just to warn you both, Milly is my husband's spy. She will report everything back to him so be very careful what you say in front of her. The poor girl will be beaten if she does not obey him.'

There was no time to speak further as the hurrying footsteps could be heard coming closer.

That evening as Ela helped Isolde undress she glanced at the reflection of the woman who had chosen to look after her many years ago.

'Maudie must live in a state of unease knowing her every move is watched by those who serve her. I can scarce imagine how much more difficult my life would have been had you not been at my side.'

Ela paused from brushing the thick, dark tresses, 'Indeed!' She exclaimed and smiled as she continued with her task.

'Well at least you are beginning to realise that your life at Wigmore was not nearly as arduous as it could have been.'

'No! I cannot imagine how Maudie copes with such a situation. I fear I would have fallen foul of Sir Philip's wrath very quickly. Do you think he beats Maudie?'

'I do not think so! Maudie may look compliant but she is the granddaughter of a Mortimer and I am sure she would have found a way of letting someone know if she had been physically abused.'

'Then let us make this visit the happiest we can and enjoy the days together without giving the maid any reason to give Sir Philip a damning report. At least we can speak our real thoughts when she is abed, or given some task which will take her out of our hearing,'

With that, Isolde rose, kissed Ela on the cheek and ran and jumped into bed.

'God's blessing on you my dearest Ela and thank you for being my guardian angel. I know I am not the easiest person in the kingdom to love but maybe one day, I will be worthy of your devotion.'

Ela left the chamber feeling that Isolde had finally begun to appreciate that love is given and not demanded and a gift to be cherished and nurtured. However, Ela was perfectly aware that Isolde could change as quickly as a sudden squall so did not set too much store by her words. All she could hope for was that over time, the lessons of life would be learned by her wayward protégé and the road of adulthood would not find her wanting.

The few short weeks the young Mortimer girls spent together were the happiest for some years but all too soon, the days drew closer to the parting. The sojourn had been of benefit to both Isolde and Maud and on the final evening as they sat quietly reflecting on the past days they knew this time was precious and that it would probably never be repeated.

As Maud and her servants rode away, Isolde waved with a tear in her eye.

'Although my future is as yet unknown, I would not change it for Maud's not for a king's ransom.'

'Amen to that!' Ela said as she crossed herself and turned to follow her young mistress back into the dark grey walls of the Dower House.

CHAPTER V

Hugh de Audley dug his spurs into the flanks of his horse as he wanted to reach Wigmore before nightfall. The thought of his brother, Nicolas, making plans concerning his future without consulting him first still rankled. There was no doubt the Mortimer family were wealthy, influential and stood high in the king's regard but marriage to a Mortimer bastard was not a union he or his mother had deemed suitable. Nevertheless, as the head of the household, Nicolas was well within his rights to arrange a marriage for his younger brother and so with mixed feelings, the young nobleman urged his tiring steed into the gathering gloom.

As the first thin rays of the moon began to split the dark heavens, Hugh de Audley and his retinue rode through the gates of Wigmore. Grooms ran forward to take the weary horses to the stable block whilst the small company of attendants headed by their master, were ushered into the Great Hall. The company fell silent as Edmund Mortimer, Lord of Wigmore, rose and moved forward with a broad smile.

'We were beginning to think it would be morrow before you arrived. Come and partake of some refreshments before you wash off the dust of the roads.'

Hugh took the proffered hand of his host and looked round at the seated figures spying the loose, limbed frame of his brother leaning back on his chair with a half smile flickering on his lips.

Hugh nodded in his direction but it was obvious to the onlookers the relationship between the de Audley brothers was not a close one. Beside Nicolas sat his wife, Katherine Giffard who was a handsome woman, her expression betraying none of her personal misgivings at the re-union of the two siblings.

After the initial lull, the company quickly began to chatter and the moment of tension melted, at least for the time being. Hugh and his attendants were shown to their apartments so they could wash and change their stained travelling clothes.

A short while later they rejoined the guests of Lord and Lady Mortimer. Edmund beckoned Hugh and turned to the seated figure of his half sister Isolde.

'Come, let me present the Lady Isolde.'

Hugh bowed and took the proffered hand of his wife-to-be and raised it to his lips although made no actual contact. The dark eyes of the young widow did not flinch under his intense gaze.

'It has been a long time since last we met, Lady Isolde.'

She looked bemused. 'I do not remember a previous meeting with you my Lord.'

'I was my late brother William's squire but then you were still little more than a child.'

'And you must have been much of an age my Lord?'

Isolde did not lower her gaze and he quickly realized by her manner, this Mortimer girl was nothing like the gentle Anabilla de Quincy, his late wife.

'You and your family have suffered a series of losses in recent years for which you have my deepest condolences.' Her voice dropped. 'I too have been bereaved by tragic circumstances and know the pain it causes.'

'Death walks amongst us unhindered, I fear but we must trust in God's will.'

Isolde continued to look up at the speaker and felt there was a double meaning to his response but merely nodded in agreement. The evening progressed in a friendly atmosphere, knights and squires, lords and their Ladies enjoyed the relaxing atmosphere and the anticipation of the forthcoming wedding festivities.

However, for the bride, the evening was one of uncertainty and misgivings; Hugh de Audley was a well set, and for some, would be described as handsome but Isolde had detected a coldness in the depths of his light, hazel eyes which left her with a sense of foreboding.

Upon retiring to her chamber, she voiced her fears to Ela who listened intently.

'It is too early to judge, remember, he must also have his misgivings about this marriage.'

'Mmm! I do not doubt it but somehow ....' her words trailed off and Ela knew she was troubled. 'He has the look of the hunter about him.'

'Surely that is due to his colouring, russet brown hair and hazel eyes? But - it is up to you to set the tone of your relationship, state your fears openly and see what response you get! Over the last few months, I have watched you grow from girl to young woman and you are possessed of all the attributes to make a sound judgement on the matter. All I can advise you is, tread warily; how you set the foundations for your relationship is of paramount importance in these first few days and saying little may prove a better option at this point but I know you often ignore advice however, in this instance, I beg you take heed.'

Isolde caught Ela's hand.

'As ever, you are my true friend and I will *try* and take your advice and stay silent for the present at least.'

True to her word, Isolde showed she could be discreet when necessary, something she had discovered through her recent trials and Ela was pleased that the once wayward child continued her progress into maturity. She too watched the young couple and hoped their relationship would develop into a true bond not only of duty but also of mutual parity. Security was what Isolde needed to complete her life and Ela prayed that in this marriage she would find that elusive element.

A few days later, watched by friends and members of the Mortimer household, Isolde and Hugh made their vows. The festivities, which followed were boisterous and noisy, thunderous laughter rang round the rafters and ashlar walls of Wigmore. The couple had requested that the ritual of 'bedding the couple' be dispensed with, as they had both been married before and felt it was somewhat demeaning under the circumstances.

Their wishes were respected, however, the guests insisted they accompanied the young couple to the door of their apartment, which they did laughing and jesting. Finally, with the raucous voices fading, the young couple faced each other in the flickering rush light.

Isolde felt nervous as Hugh walked towards her; the dancing flames highlighted his hair and eyes and she caught her breath; the fox, that is what he reminded her of but in that instance she was determined not to become his prey, not tonight, not ever. 'Shall we toast each other and make a wish for our future life together?' She tried to keep her voice steady and light.

'If you feel the need for such trivia!' he exclaimed.

'So you think this marriage but trivial?'

'I did not seek this match, in fact, both I and my mother voiced our objections but my brother chose to ignore our wishes.'

The bluntness of his statement caught Isolde off guard and she gasped but quickly regained her composure. In lowered tones, 'it is obvious the stigma of my birth is what you and your mother objected to no doubt, and not the size of my dowry.'

The two now faced each other like combatants not husband and wife. Hugh realised that although Isolde was but slight and at least half a head shorter, she showed not a vestige of fear, unlike the ill fated Anabilla. '

'Your brother is less censorious and obviously sees a practical need for this match. Be assured, I am perfectly happy to have this marriage annulled, in fact, if I am honest, would prefer that outcome rather than serve as the de Audley brood mare.'

Her words hit the air like slivers of ice. He saw the cold fire in her dark eyes and without any preamble reached and grabbed her and pulled her to him kissing her hard on the lips. She fought him off and hit out with all of her might catching him just on the point of his chin knocking him off balance and he fell in a heap on the bed. Suddenly, she heard him laughing at first a chortle then, uncontrollably until breathless he looked up at her and said, 'e gad, by all the saints and martyrs, I've married a hell bat!.'

'No!' a bastard,' she said.

Again he began to chuckle. 'Maybe my brother thought I needed a challenge.'

'It is more likely he wished you and your mother to eat your pompous pride.'

'Come, wife lets continue this contest in bed for you have aroused my passions.'

Isolde did not move. 'If I am to join you there will be rules to this 'contest' and forfeits for the one who breaks the rules.'

'It gets better! My lance against your ....?'

'Oh no, I make the rules and you......'

Before Isolde could say more Hugh de Audley had reached over caught her hand and pulled down onto the rich coverlets beside him.

'Come Isolda, be my wife, and I vow to defend your honour from all comers.'

'Including your mother?'

He grinned. 'Including my mother.'

She studied his face for a moment to see if he was jesting. 'I hope you do not forget that promise as it seems you have already forgotten my name.'

'No! Isolde sounds so ......harsh on the ear I prefer Isolda; do you object?'

She shook her head. 'If that is what you wish to call me then so be it!'

The following morning when the young couple joined the company of guests and family it was obvious, they were far more at ease with each other and there were many nudges and winks that the coupling had been successful. For Isolde, she had reason to be triumphant as in the tussle when she had in fact lost her virginity; she had managed to hide that truth from her young husband. Ela had burned the stained nightshift and with it the fear of being discovered and now her first marriage would never again be challenged.

A few days later, the couple rode away from Wigmore but her erstwhile patroness, the dowager Lady Mortimer, had assured Isolde that if she ever needed help then the Mortimer family were always at hand should she need them. As Isolde rode beside her husband, she felt more confident of her future and had confided as much to Ela who had helped her dress that morning.

Upon their arrival Isolde looked at the mellow stonewalls of Stratton Castle with admiration and her sense of optimism increased; the stark residence of her Balun dower house banished forever to the depths of her consciousness. Here, she would make a new home and a new life for herself and her husband.

CHAPTER VI

Life for Isolde quickly settled down to a domestic routine, although the shouts of knights and squires interspersed with clashes of steel could be heard mingled with the household chatter of the servants but somehow the urgency she had experienced at Wigmore was no longer present. Surprisingly, Hugh had proved to be a considerate husband and demonstrated his appreciation of the changes she had wrought throughout their home since her arrival with little gifts. Colourful tapestries now graced the walls and bright, warm cushions were scattered on the settles, chairs and window seats. Wall light holders had been burnished which enhanced the candlelight and bowls of fresh herbs and flowers decked the dark polished chests and trestle and the floor rushes were liberally sprinkled with dried lavender seeds. Isolde had taken charge of the household with ease and was enjoying her position as mistress of Stratton.

A few months after her arrival Isolde discovered she was pregnant and her condition filled her with both pride and apprehension. Ela gave her words of comfort, and when Hugh learned he was to be a father, he was overjoyed. Pregnancy was not easy for Isolde and she found her bouts of morning sickness and lethargy frustrating. The months for Isolde, seemed interminable but soon passed and after a painful labour, she gave birth to a healthy son who they named James.

At the christening, even the imperious Dowager, Lady Ela de Longespée, appeared satisfied although the chilly atmosphere between mother and daughter-in-law remained unchanged. Isolde overheard her say, 'well, at least she has fulfilled her purpose.' Even these words did not dim Isolde's joy and triumph and for the first time in her life, she found a love beyond measure and knew she would happily lay down her life for this little bundle of humanity.

'See, he has your colouring!' she exclaimed as she looked up into the eyes of her husband.

'Well, the de Audleys copper hair, at least.'

Just then, Nicolas de Audley strolled over and looked down at his tiny nephew.

'I wish you God's bounties, free of human tribulations.'

Isolde looked up at him and smiled.

'That was well said and I thank you most sincerely.'

Nicolas nodded.

'I have recently learned Kate is with child again hence, her absence as she is unwell.'

'The discomforts are many but the reward..........is great!'

Hugh had stood by watching his wife and brother in silence. Isolde looked expectantly towards her husband.

'Well! Are you not going to thank your brother for his kind sentiments?'

Hugh shrugged.

'If it was honestly said then of course I thank him. However, I know my brother and anything that related to me has, in the past, been treated as of little value.'

'My Lord - that sounds so unkind besides, today is *not* the day to fuel uncharitable thoughts methinks.'

Nicolas de Audley shrugged.

'My brother has yet to learn when I jest and when I am serious but I am pleased to see at least his wife has the wit to see truth when spoken.'

Without another word, Nicolas de Audley turned on his heels and walked swiftly away from the couple.

'Oh Hugh! If there is one thing I learned in the Mortimer household it was that however difficult relationships are within a family, loyalty, was never found wanting. It is the glue that cements blood ties and in these uncertain times it is essential to have that allegiance to rely on.'

'You know nothing of the relationship between my brother and me.'

'Maybe not but, today, for your son's future, I beg you make peace whatever the origins of the dispute are. Believe me I understand all too well how spite and misunderstandings can grow out of all proportion, that any little perceived slight can add so that a feeling of resentment grows into hatred. Just because you and Nicolas have opposing personalities does not mean that the bond of brotherhood is not buried deep within you both.'

She paused, letting her words take effect.

'If an assassins blade were to strike at Nicolas, would you not leap to his aid?'

Hugh tried to walk away but Isolde caught his sleeve.

'If the answer to that question is no – and you would not defend your own flesh and blood then I fear there is no hope of a reconciliation and I am saddened that our son may lose an uncle who he may need in the future.'

Isolde let go of the rich woollen sleeve of her husband's tunic and turned to walk away but Hugh stepped quickly to bar her way.

'Does that mean you judge me as a poor father?'

'No! but a misguided one. What will it take to heal this rift between you? We both know that since the death of the Scots king in '86, there is unrest in the North and Nicolas has only recently returned with the King from Gascony, a region which has always proved problematic and war is commonplace; it would grieve me if aught befell either of you, thus leaving this matter unresolved. Pray, to whom should I turn if you were slain, none other than your brother. He would hold sway over our family therefore, I urge you to consider that when you utter your next barb or brush off his words of kindness to our son. Whatever it was that started this enmity between you, let it end here, today, at the christening of our son.'

'Isolde speaks the truth.' Edmund Mortimer had been standing close by and overheard the exchange between husband and wife.

'Our King is a warrior, our Marcher families raised on war but it is only with the staunch support of each family member in times of hardship that the Marcher barons have survived. My sister can see this boyhood animosity is fruitless and achieves naught. So I also urge you to take heed of her words of wisdom.'

He bowed and walked away without giving either a chance to say anything further.

'Edmund is level headed and well respected by all who know him. He speaks out of concern not only for your relationship with your brother but knowing that in an emergency he could rely on you both to work together without rancour.' She paused. 'I know how hard it will be to bow your will but if not for me, then do it for our son or, for the unity of the Marchers.' Without waiting to hear his response, Isolde turned and walked back into the throng of guests.

Later that evening, Hugh de Audley thumped his wine goblet onto the trestle table in front of him and called for silence.

'My wife and I wish to thank all of you who have come to celebrate the christening of our beloved son, James and for all your generous gifts.' He looked down at Isolde as he spoke and smiled. 'I would also like to take this opportunity to ask my brother Nicolas, if he will be generous enough to accept my heartfelt apologies for my past churlish behaviour and to consign all my former ill will to the past and from this time forward rebuild the bond of brotherhood.'

All eyes turned to look at Nicolas to see his response.

With a broad grin lighting up his face, he raised his wine cup. 'I'll drink to that with all my heart, brother.'

A great roar went up around the hall and at a signal from Hugh, the musicians struck up a lively tune and the guests returned to the serious business of merrymaking. Nicolas made his way to where his younger brother and his wife were sitting and slapped the former lightly on the shoulder.

'At last you have come of age.' He took Isolde's hand and kissed it.

'You have wrought a change in my brother I have longed to see. I hope our children will grow up in friendship and amity.'

Isolde clapped her hands together, 'I believe this bodes well for our son and for the de Audley brothers.' She rose and kissed Hugh on the cheek. 'My especial thanks to you, my dear, for putting the needs of our son before your own pride. You have earned my undying gratitude.'

Nicolas grinned. 'Our mother will have difficulty in believing this occasion.'

Hugh raised his cup and toasted his brother. 'I am no longer a callow youth but have responsibilities of both husband and father and am beginning to realise that they should take precedence. Whatever differences we inherited through the difficult relationship between our mother and father on my part will forever be consigned to the past, on that you have my word.'

'Amen to that!' Nicolas held up his wine cup and then turned and the two brothers raised their silver vessels in a private toast.'

The following morning many rose with heavy heads and churning stomachs but not so Isolde and her husband, for their night had been filled with ardent lovemaking and the couple faced the future with a feeling of mutual optimism. Hugh hummed a little tune as he dressed for the hunt and leaned down to kiss his wife. 'You can meet us later this morning, sweeting, I will instruct the falconer to remain and await your instructions.'

'Mmm! That sounds like a good idea as I feel quite ....'

'Satisfied?' Hugh said mischievously.

'I will meet you at noon near the wood and spend an hour with the hawks then back for refreshments.'

Isolde stretched as she spoke, 'Do not forget to see our son before you leave.'

'No doubt with all the activities of yesterday he will still be asleep.'

'Not if he has inherited his father's restlessness.' They both smiled and Hugh made an exaggerated bow as he left. In the passageway, he passed Ela who dropped a neat curtsey.

'Your mistress is awake.'

Ela noted his relaxed expression; this marriage was proving to be everything Ela had wished for Isolde. When she entered the chamber, Isolde was already out of bed and sitting before the silvered mirror.

'Oh! Ela, last night was .... quite, quite wonderful! I never thought I could be so happy.'

Ela picked up the brush and began to tease out the tangles from the thick, black tresses.

'Enjoy and treasure this time for it will be a memory you will always share with each other and I pray that your joy grows stronger as each year passes.'

Isolde reached up and caught Ela's hand and squeezed it.
'You understand; is this how you once felt?'

Ela's face held a wistful expression for an instant. 'Yes, I knew the joys and sadness that love brings but – that was a long time ago and I refuse to be maudlin on this joyous morning.'

'Will you ever tell me the name of your lover?'

'No! It would serve no good purpose and I prefer to lay his memory to rest for it still causes me much heartache when I recall those times.'

'Then I will desist and never ask again.' But Isolde was determined to find out the identity of Ela's mystery lover one day.'

The rest of the celebrations continued in good spirits and all that attended went away with the feeling of well being, especially Nicolas, the Lord de Audley. It was essential for the discipline of his army that his brother would accept his command without challenge. Nicolas was certain that Hugh would be sent to serve in his cavalry when the time came and he felt that time was drawing ever closer.

Since the death of the Scottish king, Alexander, and subsequently, his heir, the Maid of Norway, the rightful succession to the Scottish throne had been hotly disputed and there was no doubt, Edward Plantagenet would not allow the bickering to continue indefinitely. Edward had intimated that of the thirteen contestants for the throne, he would support the learned and respected, John Baliol. Time would bear witness if Baliol possessed a personality forceful enough to hold the fractious lairds of the Highlands and Lowlands to order. However, the events in Scotland were to be brought to a head far sooner than anyone had imagined when in late October 1292, Robert Burnell, Bishop of Bath and Wells and Chancellor of England, died at Berwick whilst negotiating the terms of the succession with the Scots.

The death of Edward's long time friend and supporter now left the floodgates of his ambitions wide open and those close to the English king knew that grief did nothing to quell the Plantagenet temper. In less than two years, he had lost his Queen, Eleanor of Castile his mother, Eleanor of Provence and now, Robert Burnell; their voices of reason silenced forever so, there would be no curb on Edward's plans to take the Scottish throne for himself. Baliol would quickly realize he had been chosen because it was the will of the English King and thus, indirectly, it would be his iron hand controlling the matters of the State in Scotland.

As Nicolas de Audley stood and pondered on the future, and of how the ambitions of the Plantagenet King would affect his family. Meantime in Shropshire, the news of Burnell's death was to change the life of Maud FitzAlan, now Lady Burnell, forever. The fact that her husband, Sir Philip, who was heir to the vast wealth of the dead Bishop, would now put an end to the worry about their ever mounting debts.

It had been a sad year for Maud, in the dying months of winter, she had learned of her mother's illness, followed by the news of her death; then in early autumn, her sister-in-law, Alicia de Saluzzo, Richard's wife had died. Once again, she must prepare to travel to attend a funeral, this one being in the cathedral at Wells, in Somerset, where she would accompany her husband to the state funeral of their benefactor, the Bishop.

Maud wrote to her kinswoman, Isolde, detailing her melancholic state after so many family losses in such a short space of time. As she sealed the missive, she smiled sadly, no doubt, Isolde would reply stating the benefits of the last death and that Robert Burnell had lived a life of service to his king, country and the church. As Chancellor he had ensured the changes the king had instigated, many had already been fulfilled successfully, changes which would continue to benefit the nation throughout the years to come. It was true; Robert Burnell had proved his worth on many occasions and when Edward had gone on Crusade in 1272, was one of the five Regents chosen to rule England after the death of Henry III, together with her own grandsire, the late Sir Roger Mortimer. During this period, the two men had virtually run the country for more than two years after the deaths of two of the other Regents, the Earl of Cornwall and Sir Philip Bassett.

Maud sighed, the world was changing fast and she felt somewhat apprehensive but she knew her immediate task was to make ready for the long journey to Wells and the thought of the mud sodden roads filled her with dread.

CHAPTER VII

1294

Isolde dropped the letter she had received that morning, rose from her desk and went and looked out of the window. Down below on the green sward, she watched her son James, playing with his nurse-maids and her new born baby, Hugh, sleeping peacefully in a wicker crib. Life and death the great enigma. She sighed, so Maudie was a widow, no doubt a relief for her kinswoman and she turned and walked back to her desk and penned a letter of condolence although she knew there was no condolence required. She sighed again, the first flush of happy married life had soon faded most notably after her husband had returned from his first deployment under the command of his brother. Isolde recalled his words.

'I am not cut out for military service. The cut and thrust of the tourney is exciting, immediate but the long marches through the unceasing rain ....' he had finished the sentence with a snort of derision. 'How Nicolas remains so equable through it all is beyond me and where we differ. Now it looks as though the king is making ready to make war with France!'

Isolde had tried to comfort him.

'It is your duty to ....'

'I know, but still it fills me with such anger. Why does Edward wish to subjugate the Scots? We lived quite equably until Alexander's death a few years ago.'

'Maybe it is because the king feels threatened; he has quelled the Welsh – well almost! Maybe he wishes to bring Scotland under his rule and by so doing make England a stronger power.'

'And you think the way he is going about it will endear him to the Scottish people? Egad, Isolda, would you willingly bend your knee to a king who is showing little regard for their parliament under the guise of being a mediator?'

'No of course not......and I can see how it upsets you.....'

'Oh! My dearest wife, are you blind? I fear where it will all lead to – a former independent nation will not roll over and allow an English King to take their throne. John Baliol may be a man of learning and peace but Edward's high handedness will cause even the mildest of men to rebel and then watch the carnage that will bring about.'

'Nevertheless, you must obey the king's orders or die. Pray, go and seek solace with Father Melor, I have found he is full of wisdom and .....'

'You are right, I need to make penance for.....'

Isolde had threaded her hand through his arm and said softly,

'You are home now and here you can find comfort. Put aside your fears and lay down your sword and come and see our sons.'

The words of comfort had fallen upon deaf ears and two days after he had arrived, Hugh left abruptly to visit his mother, leaving Isolde feeling hurt with the niggling doubt that the man, who had left for Scotland, was not the same one who had returned. Her fears proved to be well founded for, after he arrived back home from the visit to his mother, he had been morose, short-tempered and even more restless than ever. Nothing Isolde tried to do, helped, in fact, he began to vent his frustrations on her head and Ela watched with a heavy heart as Isolde began to retaliate with sharp retorts, much slamming of doors and raised voices. There were definite echoes of the shrewish child, which were fast re-appearing, only now, with far more venom, and the whole household suffered from this new turn of events. It was therefore somewhat of a relief when Hugh received orders to return to duty and rode away from Stratton Castle.

Slowly, Isolde's ire began to dwindle. She resumed her role as chatelaine with a more subdued demeanour. Ela encouraged her to seek solace in her music and to spend more time with her growing sons. The remedy began to work its magic and a few months later Isolde appeared to have overcome her lapse. However, Ela, who knew her better than anyone else, could sense that Isolde had been deeply hurt by the change in her husband.

§

The tall, elegant figure of Maud Burnell stood and looked at her reflection in the mirror. Gone were the widows weeds, Milly knelt and straightened the dark blue kirtle.

'There, that looks better. I thought the pretty ribbon at the hem just brightened it up.'

Maud studied the effect. 'Mmm! You are right it does, and thank you. It will be good to sit at my brother's table and know we will no longer be watched.'

'I still jump at times before I remember Sir Philip is no longer in this world.'

Maud smiled. 'A relief for us both, is it not?'

'Aye my lady.'

'Do we know any of my brother's guests this evening?'

'I only know there is a Scottish Earl among the number. His manservant tried to take liberties but was quickly made aware that his advances were unwelcome and I think he was somewhat abashed after the rebuff.'

'Then let us hope the servant is not following his master's manners.'

With a final pat of her headdress, Maud prepared to leave the comfortable chamber and take her place as hostess for her brother, a natural move now they were both widow and widower.

The Great Hall was already filling with nobles, Richard rose and came forward to greet his sister and introduce her to the colourful gathering. He waved his hand and the servants hurried forward with steaming dishes of salmon, spicy pies and a variety of meats. A lone minstrel strummed some harmonious chords and snatches of popular tunes as the guest talked and ate with relish.

As the evening progressed, Maud sensed she was being watched. She glanced across to where the Scottish Earl sat. Unabashed he did not lower his gaze but inclined his head slightly and smiled. Not wishing to draw attention to herself, Maud lowered her eyes and concentrated on her food. Later, when the trestles were removed, and the evening's entertainers entered, the dark eyed figure moved to Maud's side.

'Forgive me, Lady Burnell, but I find myself entranced by your beauty.'

Maud blushed, she had forgotten the ways of courtly behaviour during the years of her marriage and now felt somewhat unsure of herself. Seeing her discomfort, he continued.

'My name is Robert de Brus, the former Earl of Carrick.'

'Former Earl!' Maud could not keep the surprise from her voice.

'I renounced my title for expediency.' He paused then whispered softly. 'I did not wish to swear fealty to John Baliol who was chosen by King Edward and crowned, so now bears the title of 'King of Scotland'.'

Maud turned to study her companion. They were much of a height but he was some thirty or so years her senior. She noted his once black hair was thickly sprinkled with grey; there were lines around his dark eyes, which twinkled with admiration and his wide lipped mouth was edged by a neat greying beard. This Scottish nobleman had undoubtedly once been a very handsome man in his youth.

'So you are Robert de Brus, Earl of Carrick and Lord of Annandale.'

'At your service, my Lady.' His warm admiring smile, left Maud in no doubt she had gained an admirer and the knowledge unnerved and delighted her in equal measure. His closeness made her aware of his masculinity. She had never felt so physically aware of a man before in her life.

'My Lord, I believe we have aroused the interest of my brother.'

'I have already spoken to Richard of my intentions towards you my Lady.'

Maud caught her breath, this was so sudden. She had only recently come out of mourning.

'I am a man who does not like to live alone. Like you, I have recently lost my spouse and my life is empty without the companionship of a woman. We both know, life is but a shadow, and swiftly passes. My time here maybe short but I see no reason not to make the most of it. I believe we could find both comfort and warmth in each other.' His dark eyes said far more than his words and Maud felt a quiver run down her spine.

'Your proposition has caught me off guard and I am nonplussed but, thank you for the compliment. May I give you my own thoughts on the matter after I have digested your proposal?'

His smile broadened, 'Of course, as long as your answer is, 'yes.'

He took her hand and drew it through his arm, 'come let us join in with the evening's merriments.'

Maud sat watching the mummers and jongeleurs but her mind was racing. Marriage was the last thing that had been on her mind when she had accepted Richard's invitation to bring her children to stay with him, this unlooked for proposal was so unexpected. Long after the guests had retired to bed, Maud lay awake, her thoughts racing. Marriage would give her prestige and although Robert had stated he had renounced his title as Earl of Carrick, it was still how he was styled as his son had not been recognized, as yet. In the darkness Maud tried to envisage her life as Countess of Carrick. It would mean she would have to leave England for her new home would be in the heart of Scotland, many, many leagues from her family, friends and former life. Was she ready to make such a drastic change? At least, in this match, it would be her choice, unlike her first, unhappy marriage to Sir Philip Burnell, a marriage of convenience arranged by her brother. Another fact popped into her train of thought, if she did not accept this offer of marriage it would leave her open to be matched with the King's choice and he would not care how it may affect her personally.

The following morning, Maud made her way to her brother's study and found him already surrounded by scribes and messengers.

'Forgive my intrusion but I must speak with you urgently.'

Richard FitzAlan looked up and noted the serious expression on his sister's face. He waved his hand and immediately the chamber cleared.

'So what is so important to bring you here at this time in the morning?'

'I have lain awake all night pondering on the Lord Carrick's proposal and wish to hear of your thoughts.'

Without any preamble, Richard looked hard at his sister before making his reply.

'You know, of course, that John Baliol has refused to assist the King in the planned invasion of France. Not a good start to his reign and knowing that Edward Plantagenet does not easily forgive or forget slights at any level, I can foresee a very difficult future inasmuch as there could be wars both in France and eventually, in Scotland.'

Maud gasped. 'Do you think it would come to that?'

'Most certainly. Edward is never afraid to fight for what he wants and believe me – he wants Scotland.'

Richard stepped forward and took his sister's hands in his.

'First, you must ask yourself if such a situation did arise where your loyalties would lie – here in England or with your new husband in Scotland.'

She looked up into his eyes, 'But Carrick is the King's man, surely?'

'My dearest Maud, remember, of the three leading claimants to the Scottish throne, your suitor has an undisputed right by birth. Consider carefully, if John Baliol continues to defy the wishes of the King, how long do you think he will remain on Scotland's throne?' He waited for his words to sink in before continuing. 'Such a situation would undoubtedly cause unrest between the nobles of Scotland and at the heart of this could be your husband and his family. At this time, Carrick is loyal to the English King but ....' he paused. 'Under such circumstances, I foresee a conflict of loyalties; especially if Carrick decides [for his son's sake], to pursue his birthright. Given that scenario, the King would rightly judge that act as treason; his rage would know no bounds, and his wrath reign would down mercilessly on those he viewed as his enemies. Therefore, the outcome would place you in jeopardy. So, consider where your loyalties would lie in such an event.'

Maud pulled her hands away. 'Surely, you are being too pessimistic; I do not see any reason to doubt the loyalty of the Earl, besides, his son is one of Edward's most trusted knights.'

She paused and looked into his eyes. 'With all your misgivings why do you not forbid this marriage?'

'Because I know how unhappy you were with Burnell and feel you should have a chance to choose your own husband this time.'

Maud's expression softened at his words.

'I cannot, or will not, share your dour predictions. Besides, when Alexander was on the Scottish throne, there were amicable relationships between the two nations, why not so again?'

Richard cleared his throat. 'We know the untimely death of Alexander, followed so quickly by the death of his granddaughter, created a void in the line of succession and with so many conflicting claims, Edward took the role of mediator and eventually supported John Baliol. He saw his choice as the man most likely to submit to his will and, thus, rule by proxy. But Baliol, who is acknowledged as being a quiet, learned man, has now chosen *not* to support the war with France, thus thwarting Edward's plans, which gives a whole new look to the Scottish situation. Edward will never allow him to wield such powers against him, mark my words.'

Maud shook her head. 'Methinks, you overstate the matter and whatever happens, I believe Carrick will remain loyal.' She stepped forward, stood on her toes and kissed her brother's cheek.

'You have helped me clarify my thoughts and I *have* now made my mind up and will marry the Earl of Carrick once he has obtained a licence from the King.' Without further ado, she turned on her heel and left. Maud did not see the deep frown, which furrowed her brother's brow as she left or know of his feelings of disquiet her announcement had caused him.

A few short weeks later Maude stood at the altar beside Robert de Brus and made her vows watched by a few members of their respective families. Maude de Braose had chosen to stay away and it was her uncle, Edmund Mortimer and his wife Margaret Fiennes, who bore witness at the ceremony as representatives of the bride's family. Isolde had stood watching Maudie with a strange mixture of joy and disquiet in her heart. It had all been so immediate, hardly time for anyone to study the groom or his Scottish ancestry. Isolde was well aware of the king's role in Scotland and no one really believed he would remain as a mediator. It was merely a shrewd way of gaining his true purpose, which was to rule Scotland.

Although the ceremony was brief and the guests few, nonetheless, the celebrations were full of merriment and laughter. The food and wine flowed freely and as a consequence, the dancing, which followed, was both vigorous and lively. Maudie had never looked happier and Isolde tried to suppress her misgivings. However, when Ela was helping her undress that night, she did voice her concerns.

'He is so much older than Maudie, in fact, old enough to be her father.'

'If he makes her happy then his extra years may be a benefit. It is obvious he is smitten with her.'

'Yes – but for how long?' Isolde looked earnest as she spoke.

'Are you not judging the match by your own experience, my dear?'

'I have a strange premonition about this Scottish Earl. How loyal would he be to the king if the throne of Scotland beckoned?'

Ela looked puzzled. 'What does that have to do with the man?'

'Do you not know - he has a legitimate claim to the throne by birth?'

'I was ignorant of that fact.'

Ela fell silent as she brushed Isolde's hair and went and laid out her night shift on the ornate bed.

'Let us pray for this marriage, that it brings only joy to both of them.'

'Well, I suppose that is all we can do as the vows have been taken and the rings exchanged. Did you see the expression on the face of his son?'

'No, I could not from my position in the church.'

'For certain, it was not one of gladness. I suppose he is looking to the future and what an offspring of this union may mean for him!'

'Being the Earl's first born son – nothing. He will inherit the title and the estates and Maudie's child would be like many other younger children who will make either an advantageous marriage or enter the church.'

'No matter, the future is in God's hands and in him we must trust.'

Ela smiled. 'Amen to that! Now, God-night child and do not fret, try to get some sleep.'

She bent and kissed Isolde's brow and then quietly left. Both women oblivious to how Scotland would come to impact on their lives and the lives of nearly all the nobles and their vassals.

CHAPTER VIII

Dunbar 1296
April

The pale watery sun glinted on the lances and pikes of the English army. Hugh de Audley could see his brother's destrier Trojan, sidling and prancing at the front of the company. He felt somewhat aggrieved, as his own mount had been lamed during the assault on Berwick a few weeks ago. Now, here he was, sat on a borrowed horse waiting to see what the aging Earl of Surrey, John de Warenne would do next. The bright azure and argent banner of Surrey fluttered proudly in the Scottish April morning. The Castle of Dunbar had refused his demand to surrender. Patrick, the Earl of March was loyal to Edward but his wife, Marjorie Comyn, had remained faithful to John Baliol and had refused Surrey's demands.

The Earl had wasted little time before beginning the siege of the castle. However, a messenger had managed to slip through the English lines to seek aid from the Scottish army who were just ten miles away at Haddington. Immediately, John Baliol had dispatched John Comyn, Earl of Badenoch, to go to the aid of his sister. As they reached Spottismuir, a ridge of high ground, which overlooked the castle, it was clear they had the advantageous position.

Leaving the infantry to continue with the siege, Surrey ordered his mounted cavalry to engage the enemy. The manoeuvre meant the English had to cross the Spott Burn, thus disrupting their lines and Comyn made the fatal mistake of believing the English were in retreat.

The Scots, seeing the confusion, had rushed to attack the English but in their haste to engage they had become disorganised, giving the English knights and their troops, time to regroup. Instead of facing a disorderly army the Scots found they now faced ranks of lances, pikes, and mounted archers and cavalry.

The battle was fierce and Hugh found himself in the thick of the fighting. The screams of men and horses echoed around his head and the ground shook with the weight of the horses.

Repeatedly, he lashed to his right and left, his sword blade dripping with the blood of his enemies, until it was clear that the Scots had been defeated. Cheers mingled with the moans of the wounded and dying. When the red mist of battle had cleared from Hugh's eyes, he could see that among those captured were knights of wealth and power and later learned that the Scottish Earls of Atholl, Menteith and Ross, as well as their commander, John Comyn were amongst the prisoners. Some useful ransoms, together with the resounding victory would no doubt bring Edward more than a little satisfaction.

However, in the aftermath of the fighting came more immediate duties and Hugh watched as surgeons moved through the ranks of the fallen, binding wounds and ordering litters to carry the badly injured to the tents for further treatment. Farriers armed with sharp blades were checking all the fallen horses and those beyond help dispatched out of their misery and pain.

The power Hugh had felt coursing through his body during the battle now drained away and he signalled for his squire as he wearily dismounted his horse.

'Check he is not wounded for I can scant afford to replace him if I find I must purchase another one for myself.'

The squire grinned. 'Aye, my Lord.'

Rollo Chetwode took the slippery reins and clicked to encourage the sweating destrier to walk in the direction of the picket line. He passed Sir Nicolas de Audley coming to see how his brother had fared during the battle and bowed as they passed each other.

'Well at least this victory will please the king.' Nicolas said as he slapped Hugh on the back.

'We were lucky it could have easily gone against us.'

Hugh nodded. 'Now I understand why you relentlessly drill your knights, had they not rallied so speedily the outcome does not bear thinking about.' He looked up at his brother. 'Am I not mistaken but did Surrey not hesitate?'

'He was blindsided and his reactions are not as immediate as they once were remember his advancing years. Nevertheless, the old man gave a good account of himself, once we engaged the enemy. He lacks nought in courage.'

Hugh smiled wryly. 'I think it is a good thing you were at his side.'

Nicolas grinned. 'Spoken like a true brother. Now come, let us get some refreshments before the day grows too much older.'

Together the two knights trudged towards their tent and sent for some warming food.

In the days that followed, prisoners were sent with escorts to await ransom. The wounded were moved to more comfortable lodgings; fletchers were busy flighting arrows, blacksmiths were hammering steel for shoeing the horses and repairing the buckled armour and chain mail. Fires crackled at intervals around the campsite with tripods littering the area, bearing pots full of simmering broth. Men were recounting their part in the action as the life of the English troops continued in the age old traditions, whilst priests said mass in thanks for God's mercy in saving the day and for the souls of the dead. The lull meant there was time to write to family and friends, take stock of the losses and await the arrival of the king.

Edward Plantagenet swept into the camp with his train of followers and the celebrations began with cheers going up from all sides. That evening wine and ale flowed amid a lot of ribaldry and high spirits.

'Ah! Young Audley I hear you accounted yourself well this day.'

Hugh looked embarrassed. 'I only did what all of us did, sire, and put into practice the training of knighthood.'

The king grinned. 'But with great enthusiasm from what I have been told.'

Hugh wriggled uncomfortably in his seat.

Edward continued, 'You obviously put the lessons from your days at Windsor to good use!.

'Aye sire! Being one of the king's squires was good grounding.'

'That is good to hear! You must bring your wife to court upon our return to England.'

Hugh bowed and thanked the king in muffled tones.

As Edward turned to speak to Surrey, Nicolas nudged his brother, 'royal recognition and once at court who knows where it may lead.'

'It was merely a polite invitation, pray do not read aught into it!'

'Well no doubt Isolde will be proud of your exploits will, she not?'

'That will mean more expense with new clothes no doubt.' Hugh sounded disgruntled.

'It is a great honour to be personally invited to court by the king you should bear that in mind. Now drink up and enjoy your moment of glory.'

In the weeks that followed the victory at Dunbar, the castles of Roxburgh and Stirling surrendered, together with many others. John Baliol realised the Scots rebellion was all but lost and in July he capitulated. Edward seized the Scottish crown jewels, the Black Rood of Saint Margaret and the Stone of Scone. The latter was not only a symbol of power but had been used in the crowning of Scottish kings for centuries.

In August, the Scottish nobles and magnates assembled to swear allegiance to the English king who produced a document for each to sign, but also to add their personal seals, blatantly demonstrating his doubts as to their sincerity. The manuscript was dubbed the 'Ragmans Roll', the final humiliation of his enemies. Leaving trusted commanders in control, Edward and the rest of the army returned to England in the belief that the wars with Scotland were at an end. However, a number of seasoned campaigners were filled with misgivings, and their fears increased as they journeyed back to England as they passed through ruined villages, scorched fields and devastated crops and saw the hatred and resentment in the faces of the people who eyed them with suspicion as they rode by. It would take but a spark to reignite this conflict and they would not have to wait long for this to come to fruition.

CHAPTER IX

Stanton Audley

'They should arrive within the hour.' Isolde's words hid a wealth of emotions. Did she feel pleased at the news of the imminent return of her husband or was she secretly dreading it? She fingered her rosary, which hung from her belt, praying to the Virgin Mary for forgiveness and courage.

Servants bustled busily about laying the trestle tables in readiness for the arrival of their lord and his knights and squires. There was urgency about their actions for they knew Lady Isolde wished all to be in order for the return of their lord. Fresh rushes had been scattered, sprinkled with herbs and sweet smelling flower heads. On the side trestles, vases were filled with flowers and ferns in readiness to greet the travellers.

Suddenly, the courtyard filled with men and horses, the clamour rising to the quiet solar. Isolde crossed her fingers, then made the sign of the cross as she moved towards the door. Her heart raced in trepidation at the forthcoming reunion. Hastily she hurried down the stairwell and into the Great Hall as she waited for the doors to open. She smoothed her kirtle, took a deep breath as the heavy oak doors swung back to reveal Sir Hugh and his retinue.

Isolde moved forward her hands outstretched in greeting. 'My Lord........' she stopped short, for the man before her had changed dramatically as he now sported a heavy moustache which gave him the appearance of a Viking. Ela sensed Isolde would say something unguarded and made a deep curtsey, thus distracting her mistress who had noted the warning look in her companion's eyes.

'My Lord, you are welcome home.' She gestured to the waiting servants to come forward and offer refreshments to the noisy group who had surged into the Hall.

'It is good to be back, the journey has been interminable and I fear it will take a week of bathing to rid me of the dirt of Scotland's roads.' He stepped forward and took Isolde's hands, raised them to his lips, and kissed them. As soon as we have had a little wine to lay the dust then I think we shall all need to bathe before eating.'

Isolde smiled. 'All is in readiness and hot water is being carried to your chamber as we speak.'

Without further ado, Hugh de Audley took a long draft from his cup of wine and then beckoned to his body servant to follow as he walked briskly from the throng. Isolde had noted the tiredness in his eyes and wondered whether the change in her husband was not only the silky red-gold moustache he now wore.

The evening had gone well and Isolde felt satisfied that she had pleased her husband. It did not detract from her growing apprehension at the thought of the forthcoming physical reunion. She just hoped he would be too tired and it would be but a swift coupling before he fell asleep. She had been correct in her assumptions and after the urgent onslaught of his lust, he quickly fell asleep leaving Isolde feeling used and resentful. How long she lay there lost in her thoughts she was uncertain but was soon disturbed by the moans and grunts of the sleeping man. Suddenly, with his arms flaying the air, he roared obscenities, grabbed Isolde by the hair and began to attack her as though he wanted to kill her. With all her strength she fought back crying out in pain and anguish.

'Get off me you great brute!' She managed to strike him hard in the face and the groin thus waking him and as he slowly began to gather his senses, a look of horror replaced the one of fury.

'God forgive me!'

'I think you should first ask my forgiveness as I am the one who will bear the marks my lord.'

Hugh bowed his head and tried to take her in his arms but she pushed him away and rose and left the bed.

'You have returned a monster, my lord, and I for one will not share a bed with you until you have quelled your demons.'

'I beg your forgiveness.' He looked forlorn, his bowed head in his hands. 'At times I am beset by nightmares so real - they engulf me!'

Isolde tossed her long hair, 'and almost engulfed me!' She returned angrily and went and sat on the edge of the bed.

'Have you sought help, my lord?'

He shook his head. 'I had not realised my dark dreams were so physical.'

'Promise me you will seek help from the physician. I am sure he can give you some calming potion.' She paused. 'If you do not then at some point you will either harm me or yourself.' She hesitated. 'Besides, carrying this terrible burden must affect your whole life.'

'I fear it has! And now it would seem yours also!'

'Was the experience so fearful it has brought you to this state?'

He raised his head and looked deep into her eyes. She could see all the torment lurking in his gaze.

'I was hailed a hero after Dunbar but no one mentions Berwick.' His voice broke. 'There were no heroes in Berwick. We killed men, women and children and the streets ran with their blood.'

Isolde made the sign of the cross then moved closer, she had quickly regained her own composure with the realisation of her husband's predicament. Slowly, she moved closer towards the hunched figure and gently placed her arm around his shoulders. 'The sin was not yours, my lord.' She said softly. 'God understands and forgives.'

Hugh looked at his wife. 'Does He?'

'Yes, if you ask Him.'

'I have felt godless, felt a complete hypocrite whence hearing Mass.'

'Father Melor will guide you with your conscience. Do you think you are the first soldier to have such feelings? War has been a way of life through the centuries and will no doubt continue through the centuries to come. God will not abandon you, not even when you abandon Him. If you cannot forgive yourself I truly believe that God will forgive you and give you absolution and peace of mind.'

'But can you ever forgive me?'

She gave a wry smile. 'A few moments ago I would have said no but now I am apprised of your wounded mind.......' She bent and kissed his hair. 'If you will let me, I will help you but only if you are prepared to take the first step in seeking help for yourself.'

He reached and grasped her hand. 'You have my vow I will do as you ask.'

'Now rest; I will sit beside you so you can sleep and on the morrow we will speak to the physician.'

After she had coaxed her husband to lie down Isolde stroked his brow until he fell asleep and she settled down to watch over him until dawn. Throughout the night, her mind ranged over all that had taken place. She had witnessed vulnerability in her husband that she had never seen before and it unnerved her somewhat. One thing she was sure of, what happened during the next few days, would define her marriage throughout the coming years. Here was a chance to prove she was both worthy of his complete trust and capable of helping him through this crisis and in so doing, forge an unbreakable bond. Once she had made up her mind to achieve this goal over the coming days, Isolde allowed herself to doze.

When the cock crowed Hugh awoke and looked across at the figure of his wife curled up in the chair. She opened her eyes.

'Good morrow my lord, did you sleep better?'

'The best I have had for many weeks.'

'Good! Then I shall call Simon to have your bath ready for when you rise. Afterwards we can discuss the best way to go forward.'

For an instance, Isolde saw an expression cross his face which made her fear he was about to resist her suggestion and she hesitated before continuing.

'But first, I know your sons are eager to see their father again. It would be a good start to the day, do you not think, my lord?'

He nodded and his face relaxed. Isolde breathed a silent sigh of relief. This was going to be a battle of wits and guile but she would not shy away from it and accepted the hidden challenge.

The suggestion had been a good one as the boys leapt about in their excitement firing questions like a hail of arrows.

'What colour was the king's charger? How many men were in his command? How long was the siege at Dunbar? Did he sleep in a tent?' How many men had he slain?'

Isolde winced at the last one and raised her hand for silence.

'Boys! Boys! Do you wish to overwhelm your sire with so many questions he will withdraw?'

'Oh, but Mama!'

'He will answer them one by one but only if you behave yourselves.'

Hugh bent on his haunches so his face was level with those of his sons.

Little Hugh looked hard at his father and said in a serious tone.

'Did you take that moustache off someone, Papa?'

'No! That is all home-grown.'

Hugh laughed aloud and Isolde rejoiced at the sound. It had been a good decision to make a visit to the nursery, although, James would soon be moving to another household in readiness to begin his training as a squire and was of a far more serious nature.

'How many leagues is Scotland from here?'

'It is many, many, hundreds and a great number of horseshoes to prove it!'

'Were you frightened?'

'Knights have to conquer their own fear before they can conquer their enemies.'

Isolde clapped her hands. 'Enough questions you must not tire your father he needs to rest and regain his strength. So off to your lessons and we will come and see you again tonight.'

As they walked from the nursery, Hugh smiled at his wife.

'They are bright and happy and I have you to thank for their wellbeing.' He paused. 'My absence made me realise what a comfortable and well run household I have and it is all due to your good management. I missed the comforts of home more than you will ever know.'

'Then I am well pleased you feel thus. I enjoy most of my duties as chatelaine at Stratton. Now come and see what I have done with the garden.'

'You have planted more fruit trees?'

'We have plenty of dry, airy cellars to keep apples, plums and pears for the winter. The medlars and quinces are made into relishes, jellies and sauces whilst the apricots are dried for a variety of uses. I have also increased the flock of hens and found it beneficial with the production of eggs and meat. By the end of winter, I for one, get thoroughly sick of salted meats and fish.'

Hugh nodded he was enjoying this hour of domesticity and he reached for Isolde's hand and kissed her fingers in turn. 'All the treasures of the world cannot be greater than to have a wife of your qualities.'

Isolde was taken aback by his words. 'I merely do my duty, my lord.'

'No, you do much, much, more, you bring calm and organisation into a chaotic world.'

Isolde smiled. 'I never thought to hear such words for I have always been judged a disruptive force throughout my childhood at Wigmore. I suppose I have grown up and now, see how little is achieved by being contrary.' She paused. 'I have spotted similar traits in our eldest son, James, but thankfully, only when he is thwarted in situations he deems unfair.'

'But not in little Hugh?'

'No. Hugh appears an affable child. He likes to look at his reflection in the mirror and we tease him and call him vain.'

'Childish habits will disappear once they begin their training to become squires.'

'Indeed!'

The couple walked back to their apartment and took some refreshment before summoning Gregory the physician. After describing Hugh's symptoms, he asked a few more questions and then rose to take his leave. 'I shall have a formula ready for you directly, my lord. There may be a few side effects such as a little dizziness on rising but if you sit for a few moments it will pass and you should feel no other abnormal signs.'

'Thank Master Gregory, I shall keep you apprised of the efficacy of your remedy.'

The little man bowed and left.

Hugh looked across at Isolde. 'Now I must go to my study and catch up on the matters of the day as I am sure you must too?' He took his wife's hand and raised it to his lips. 'I will see you later, my dear.'

For a few weeks, the life of Isolde's family settled into a pattern and she liked the rhythm of the days. Sadly, the time of peace was all too short, dashed by a messenger from the king. When Hugh de Audley stepped from his study after reading the royal message his face was grave and a frown furrowed his brow. He walked quickly to his wife's chamber where she was stitching a large tapestry; Ela was choosing silks from a woven basket.

Isolde stopped her task.

'My lord you appear disconcerted, what ails you?'

'I must make all haste to Gascony with as many men I can muster to aid the Earl of Lincoln. However, there is worse to come, the king has ordered that grain, horses and weapons be seized from all his earls and nobles – in fact, from all but the poorest, to aid his war in Gascony.'

Isolde gasped. 'Surely the king would not alienate his subjects even further?'

'I am afraid it does not end there. He has ordered the church to hand over lands and treasures for his cause.'

'Heaven preserve us!' exclaimed Isolde.

The messenger has witnessed trouble on his route with many people resisting the seizures especially when it comes to livestock. Apparently, a number of Earls are in dispute over such methods.'

'Sadly, not the Earl of Gloucester for he has fallen ill by all accounts.'

'Well it appears, Arundel, Hereford, Warwick and Norfolk are all voicing their opposition and added to the voice of the church there will be riots in his own lands, ere long, I fear.'

'How soon must you leave, my lord?'

'As soon as I can summon enough troops!' he exclaimed. His expression told Isolde all she needed to know about how he felt about this new turn of events.

'The messenger is riding on to Wigmore, to summon the Mortimers to attend a parliament. No doubt Nicolas will also be called to attend.'

'Once more we are plunged into conflict but I never thought it would be in such a manner.'

'I must write and inform all those who served me in Scotland to make ready and this time their destination is Gascony.'

The coming weeks brought hectic activity throughout Stratton and the neighbourhood. There were troops to feed and arm, horses to purchase and rations to find. Isolde was at her wits end at the extra expense and loss of not only food but also forage needed by the gathering troops. Thus leaving her household to suffer the shortfall throughout the coming winter. There were other fears Isolde felt deeply, and these were for the welfare of her husband. Master Gregory's medication had been a success and Hugh had benefitted by restful nights. How would this new turn of events affect his mindset whilst overseas? She refused to contemplate the idea he may never return, for widowhood held nothing but uncertainty and she had no wish to find herself in such a position again.

All too soon the day dawned when Hugh and his men made ready to depart and on a frosty dawning the party of men, wagons, knights and squires left the watching group of family and servants.

Isolde sighed as she made the sign of the cross as she wondered how long this deployment would be. 'Come Ela, we cannot dally in this chilly air. See the children are returned to their quarters and we will set too and take stock of what provisions we have been left with for the winter.'

CHAPTER X

January 1297

Edward Plantagenet sat facing his nobles and magnates, a thunderous expression on his face. No one was in any doubt the forthcoming meeting would be a turbulent affair.

'Sire,' Roger Bigod, the Earl of Norfolk, stood to address his liege lord. 'I will not condone this proposal to outlaw the church for their lack of support for your wars.' A rumble of agreement ran round the chamber.

'Beware Norfolk that you do not stray into the realm of treason.' Edward's voice held a menacing growl.

'Rome will never sanction your actions Sire and you yourself could stand in danger of excommunication.' Again, the hum of voices filled the air.

'If you are not with me, Norfolk, then you are against me. Who else will dare oppose me in this matter?' The ice blue eyes ranged over the assembly. Then the Earls of Arundel, Warwick and Hereford all rose as one. Edward glared at each in turn.

'Damn you to the flames of hell fire. I am your liege lord and sovereign and would you defy my summons and break faith with me?'

Richard FitzAlan, the Earl of Arundel, looked uncomfortable but held his head high as he replied.

'We have pledged our bodies in your service, Sire, but not our souls.'

The clamour that ran round the chamber was like a roll of thunder.

'So maybe you will fund these wars for your realm you misbegotten sons of ....'

'Sire!' the clear tones of Bishop Winchelsea interrupted the king's words of rebuke and rose above the garbled voices. 'If you deny men the right to speak freely, you will be deemed a tyrant and that is not what this argument is all about. The church cannot and will not subscribe to this outrageous method of claiming taxes. I have already sent word to Pope Boniface for guidance to see if he has changed his stance on this matter. Therefore, until I receive his direction I am unable to move from the position I now find myself in. Surely, you must see how my hands are tied, Sire. I answer to a higher authority than that of the King of England.'

Once more, the chamber was full of raucous voices until Edward banged his fist on the trestle table. As the company fell silent, Edward's words, venomous in their intensity, rang out and echoed to the rafters.

'So, churchman, do you think I am about to wait on a word from Rome? Would you have our enemies overrun us for want of silver? I will not wait on your Master from Rome but by all the powers, you *will* obey Edward of England.' And, without further ado, he rose and swept out of the chamber, hastily followed by his servants.

For what seemed like an age the assembly remained silent then, slowly individual voices rose to air their opinions. The Earls sat and listened for a while, then Humphrey de Bohun, Earl of Hereford, raised his hands.

'My Lords, I beg each of you to have a care and take time to consider your next move. I think we should all depart and gather to discuss this more closely when tempers have cooled and heads have cleared.'

With much scraping of chairs and mutterings, England's nobles and magnates left, some in groups, some in twos, others alone, beckoning to their waiting servants as they passed through the heavy doors.

'There will be ramifications.' Richard Fitz Alan's words were hushed as he spoke to his fellow objectors.'

Roger Bigod nodded. 'We can expect nothing less from the king. No doubt his first move will be to relieve us of our positions at court.'

'My Lords, I will keep you in my prayers for we all know how the royal rage can turn into vengeance. You must all support each other in this and remind the king of the rights set out in the Magna Carta, a document, which has stuck in the throats of at least three Plantagenet kings.'

'The Bishop is right, our only chance of success is to stand firm and hope common sense eventually prevails.'

Humphrey de Bohun shook his head. 'We all know the late Chancellor, Burnell was the only mediator Edward would listen to. His death has robbed us of an able negotiator and he is sorely missed on such occasions'

There was a murmur of assent. 'For now, we will return to our homes to ride out the Plantagenet wroth.'

'A vain hope I fear.' The Earl of Arundel's voice was flat as he shook each man's hand. 'Now we brace ourselves for the storm. God go with you all.'

The mood of the Earls was dark and when Richard FitzAlan spied Nicolas de Audley, he fell in step with him and recounted the breakdown of support for the king's proposals to outlaw the church.

'Once again the cost will fall to others. Our family is already in debt due to the wars in Wales and Scotland and now, Gascony. Where will it all end?'

'I know not, but you can wager what funds you have left, that Edward will not drop his current ambitions so we can all look to more hardships in the months to come.'

'It becomes ever more expensive to train and field our squires and the cost of destriers and chargers grows yearly plus their armour and caparisons. If we raise the subject, it is ignored, and if we do not keep our men at arms well armed it is we who will suffer on the field of battle.'

With that, the two men walked out of the royal palace to seek their respective mounts to begin their journeys home. However, within weeks, the recalcitrant Earls were summoned to attend Parliament at Salisbury where after heated debates, the members refused to uphold Edward's plans for war in Gascony. The enraged king slammed out of the chamber in high dudgeon, his face red with rage and threatening to dismiss Roger Bigod as Earl Marshal and Humphrey de Bohun as Constable of England. But the anger was not one sided and many who left Salisbury on that bleak day rode away with heavy hearts.

Nicolas de Audley turned his horse's head towards Oxfordshire determined to visit his sister-in-law on his way home. The sky was heavy with snow as he urged his mount through the mud spattered roads. It was dangerous to be caught in a strange place, footpads and robbers were not opposed to murdering any unsuspecting traveller. The wary knight gave orders for his men to keep a vigilant eye on the unfamiliar surroundings.

It was some days later they eventually arrived at Stratton and Nicolas was glad to lie in a clean bed after partaking of a tasty, warming meal. However, he was somewhat surprised that he was not the only visitor to Stratton as Maud FitzAlan, now Countess of Annandale, was also there. After the strained atmosphere at court, Nicolas found the ambiance at Stratton a welcome relief and on his second night, the music and easy banter helped him to relax. It was on the following morning he found himself alone with Isolde.

'I apologise for descending on you without prior warning. I did not expect you to have guests.'

Isolde looked up at him and smiled. 'You are always welcome here, my lord.' Her tone was sincere as she continued. 'It was somewhat of a surprise to me when I received an urgent message from Maudie. It has been a long time since we were together.'

'Nothing untoward I hope.'

There was a long pause before Isolde spoke again. 'My lord, I know I can confide in you with every confidence that nothing we speak of will go beyond these walls.' A hint of a frown furrowed her brow. He stepped forward and took her hand. 'You can always rely on me, I hope you know that.'

'Yes, I do! It is difficult to divulge another's confidences though and I do it out of true concern not only for the lady in question but …….. also for our country.' Isolde indicated to a window seat and the couple moved and sat, neither noticed the snow, which had begun to fall in thick flakes quickly covering the ground, trees and hedgerows.

'As you know, the Earl of Annandale sought the king's support in his claim to the Scottish throne but it seems after the king refused, the mood of the Earl changed and he returned to his estates in England. Since that time Maudie has noticed many messengers coming and going. She has also noticed that whenever the Earl's son, Robert, visits, they talk privately for many hours and grow silent whenever she goes nigh. She has been more than troubled by this turn of events which began when her lady-in-waiting, Milly, was raped by one of the visiting Scots. The whole incident was tragic; she discovered that she was with child and although Maudie assured her she and the child would be taken care of..........Milly subsequently hanged herself. The whole matter cast a long, dark shadow over her marriage and now she feels an outsider.'

Nicolas crossed himself. 'God have mercy on that poor girl's soul.'

'Maudie is at her wits end and does not know what to do next. If she tells her brother about the visitors, she feels she is betraying her husband but if she remains silent and there is treachery brewing then she will be judged as being a traitor to her own people.'

'It is a conundrum, for certain, but I think Arundel should be told, if not by his sister then, maybe a servant could disclose the matter of the many visits from Scotland.'

Isolde nodded. 'There is but one flaw in that plan – all the servants are Scots.'

'Mmm! I can see the problem.' He stroked his chin for a moment. 'Then why do you not request a visit and you can disclose your fears for her safety especially after the terrible death of her personal maid.'

Isolde reached over and took his hand. 'I do believe you have solved the problem. I will put the suggestion to Maudie this very morning and hope it will help to ease her conscience. Richard is resourceful and I feel sure he will resolve the whole issue and extricate Maudie from such a dangerous position.' She looked deep into her brother-in-law's face.

'Do you think Lord Annandale and his son are would be traitors?' Her words were little more than a whisper.

'I think the king has sorely misjudged the situation with not upholding their legitimate claim. Reports from Scotland state there is scant local rule and the country is becoming ever more lawless. Lawlessness spells trouble and the king will not only have his armies fully engaged in France but also in Scotland.'

'Of course, Wales has to be added to that as there are always disputes which break out into fighting even though the king believes it is a conquered nation.'

Nicolas de Audley gave a wry grin. 'Amen to that statement.'

'Pray do not mention our conversation to Maudie.'

'I had no such intention. I would never betray your trust, my Lady. Now changing the subject, have you heard from my brother recently?'

'A brief note, full of complaints but no details – which I can understand! The boys are always in his thoughts. Thankfully, they are growing like weeds but I do worry about James, as it will soon be time for him to begin his new life as a squire. Hugh mentioned he may be summoned as one of the king's household but I would much prefer him to be in a safer environment at this time.'

'Try not to cosset him too much. I know how dear he is to you both but the lessons of life have to be learned and the sooner the better. Remember, our mother coddled Hugh and he has many shortcomings because of it! Now, let us join the others.' He glanced through the window. 'It would appear you will have your guests for an extended stay as the snow is sticking and is falling thick and fast.'

'Before we go, I would ask you how does Thomas fares. Has he overcome the lung complaint?'

A look of concern flickered across the face of Nicolas de Audley. 'I fear it is a condition that not even the tender ministrations of Katherine has been able to cure. All we can do is pray that as he grows older it will diminish altogether.'

Isolde nodded and the couple rose to join the other guests at Stratton.

Five days later Nicolas and his party left, followed shortly by Maud and her entourage and life at Stratton returned to normality. However, as soon as the primroses began to flower along the hedgerows Isolde received Maudie's invitation as secretly arranged and on a bright, blustery spring morning, she left on her pre-arranged mission. Isolde felt somewhat apprehensive about her reception but she squared her shoulders and reminded herself that Mortimers faced their fears with courage and thus mentally armed, she rode through the handsome gates of manor house at Hatfield Broad Oak.

Maudie greeted her with delight. She helped her from the carriage and hugged her and then turned to hug Ela.

'Oh! I am so pleased to see you both again.' She looked around to see if they were being watched, as she squeezed Isolde's hand and whispered, 'My stepson is here with some of his 'friends'.'

'It should be an interesting meeting.' Isolde voice was quite low and calm although she felt a flutter of butterflies in her stomach. When the new arrivals entered the hall, as expected, there was a definite tension in the air and although Robert de Brus the senior, was the epitome of good manners and courtesy nevertheless, Isolde noticed the under current that permeated the grand manor house. Servants attended to their immediate needs and swiftly removed the boxes of luggage. From a doorway, a figure emerged and Isolde met Maudie's stepson, Robert de Brus the younger, for the first time. She noted the dark, grey eyes, set back in their sockets, with the unswerving gaze. His hair was thick and as black as pitch and he was taller and not as thick set as his father but there was a power, which emanated both physically and mentally. He had a deep, well modulated voice but she knew he was more than curious at her visit. With all the aplomb she could muster, Isolde tried to make light of her sudden arrival.

'Due to all our family commitments over the past few years, my dearest Maud and I, have seen but little of each other so I took the opportunity to come and visit.' Isolde raised her eyebrows. It is obvious my message of intent never arrived. I hope my visit will not be too disruptive.'

Robert de Brus, the elder, stepped forward.

'You are most welcome. I have been neglecting my wife these past months, I admit, and this diversion will make her happy, I am sure.' He beckoned a servant to bring a tray of refreshments for the guests and when it arrived he indicated. 'Please help yourself to wine and then I am sure you need to go and rest yourselves.'

Isolde thanked him and sipped at the delicious French wine. She tried to appear at ease but was glad to escape the scrutiny of the de Brus men folk.

'The younger Brus has an imposing aura and those keen eyes of his missed naught. We must be very careful what we say and how we say it throughout this visit,' she whispered to Ela as she changed her travelling attire. Ela nodded. 'I will try and gain what intelligence I can from the servants without causing suspicion.'

'I think from now on it will be wise to say nothing until we have left ....'

The two women kept to this premise throughout their five-day stay and it was not until they were well on their homeward journey that they began to speak freely of what they had seen and heard.

'I know one messenger was secreted out of the house during our visit.' Ela's voice was low, not wishing to be heard by anyone other than Isolde 'and - there was also a reluctance to talk about poor Milly. However, I did discover her rapist was a member of the Campbell clan who was sent home immediately after the crime and no one is certain whether her death was reported to him. I do know that the woman who now attends Maudie, Arianna, is from the Border country and she is loyal to her new mistress.'

Isolde sighed. 'Well at least that is something positive. As for myself, I gained nothing of great import but..........there was an evening I walked in unobserved and heard the name of Comyn mentioned in a derogatory manner. It seems they are rival claimants for the Scottish throne and all I heard was- he could not be counted on. As soon as they became aware of my presence, the conversation concluded. I feel there is need to report this to Richard. He will know what to do of that I am certain.'

Isolde sent a fast riding messenger to the Earl of Arundel to apprise him of the fears and the position his sister Maud now found herself in. His reply was short and to the point.

My dear Lady Isolde,
I warned my sister of such an outcome to her hasty marriage.
Be assured I have begun to take steps to extricate her from this
predicament.
Your obedient servant,
Richard FitzAlan

Isolde clapped her hands. 'We will have to wait and see what steps he is taking but am secure in the knowledge that Maudie's future is now in the sage hands of her brother.'

CHAPTER XI

Robert Winchelsea, Archbishop of Canterbury, sat before his scroll-strewn desk, where so many letters of complaint about the king's insistence on taxing the clergy throughout the kingdom, that not an inch of the vast desk could be seen. However, it was the letter he had opened that morning bearing the Arundel crest, which caused him to frown. He called for his secretary to cancel the rest of the morning's interviews as the matter in hand needed some careful consideration.

Arundel had couched his words carefully but the sharp-witted cleric knew full well what the letter had implied and he could see Arundel's dilemma. The Archbishop indicated to his scribe to bring a heavy volume of deeds and marriage licences pertaining to the leading earldoms of the realm. He turned the pages to the thick section on the de Clare family and began to read, and re-read a particular section until he appeared satisfied. With great deliberation, he raised his quill and with many pauses began to write the reply to the Earl's missive. Eventually, with a flourish, he signed his name, sanded and sealed the scroll before handing it to his clerk.

'See that is delivered with all haste.'

The obedient clerk hurried from the chamber to do his master's bidding.

With a shrug of his shoulders, Robert Winchelsea began to write a letter, which would change the life of Maud FitzAlan. Once again, he called for his clerk to take the finished letter to a messenger to make all speed to the home of the Earl of Carrick in Essex. Satisfied, in the knowledge that he had set in motion the first steps to end the marriage of Lady Maud FitzAlan, he took a deep breath and returned to his former task. He began to dictate a letter to his scribe that would be sent to all parishes throughout the realm giving every bishop and diocese the authority to make their own arrangements with regard to the king's persistent demands for taxes. However, he would remain unmoved and would continue to refuse the king's outrageous call for a fifth percent of the church's income. The Pope was his earthly master and he would listen to his voice and not bow to the ambitions of a Plantagenet king.

In Arundel Castle, a breathless messenger ran up the stone stairwell and knocked on the stout, dark oak timbered door. A liveried page answered; the messenger thrust the scroll into his hand and stood back awaiting further instructions. Dutifully the page handed the scroll to his master. Richard FitzAlan read the message and a wry smile curved his lips in satisfaction.

'Good! Excellent, I knew I could rely on the Archbishop to resolve this matter.'

He spoke aloud to no one in particular but seemed well pleased as he continued with his own affairs. The marriage of his sister was to be annulled – the reason, consanguinity. It mattered, not a jot, to the Earl what reason was to be used. The church would ensure the marriage was ended and that was all he had wished for, besides, any blame from the Brus family would be aimed squarely at the church, with not a hint of suspicion falling on anyone else's head.

No doubt, Maud would return to Arundel but he felt relieved at the outcome of the whole business. Once Maud was under his roof, he could ensure that she did not undertake any more risqué relationships.

However, in early June all thoughts of personal matters faded upon learning the dire news from France. Edmund Plantagenet, brother of the king, and Earl of Lancaster, had died. A few weeks later further bad tidings arrived. Henry de Lacy, Earl of Lincoln and the English army had been defeated. Details stated that the English forces had been outnumbered, many had deserted as they had received no wages since landing in France. Those who had remained loyal to the crown had faced the French but were outnumbered and the depleted force had scant option but to surrender. Henry de Lacy, together with the other nobles were now prisoners of the French.

The atmosphere at court had been heavy with grief but with the news of the defeat now became toxic. Edward Plantagenet was incensed. He turned his rage on the church who had refused to support his war in France. Now he had lost his brother and his good friend de Lacy was held in prison with a number of others to ransom. His ire was terrifying in its intensity.

In Oxfordshire, Isolde was sitting in her solar, a stunned expression etched across her features.

'Mercy, how do they think I am to raise such a sum?'

Ela reached across and held her hand. 'Do you know whether Lord Nicolas is apprised of this ransom demand?'

Isolde shook her head. 'I have no notion. Maybe his mother would help. I cannot bear the thought of moneylenders but if that is the course I have to take then so be it!'

'I'm sure it will not come to that, the de Audley family name is a respected one and there will be supporters who will come to your aid.'

Isolde smiled sadly. 'Oh! Ela, I am not so sure, with all the extra taxes and the king's commissioners seizing goods and livestock, there is precious little goodwill at this time.'

'Then why not seek help from the Mortimers? After all they are your blood family.'

Isolde's face clouded. 'I never truly felt part of that family although I have been treated better than most bastard offsprings. No! I will try to resolve this myself, after all, I am his wife and therefore it should fall to me to find sufficient funds to fulfil the ransom demand.

However, it was Nicolas de Audley, who wrote to Isolde and informed her that he had sold lands and when arrangements could be made, the ransom would be met. Isolde was moved to tears upon reading his words.

'Lord Nicolas never fails in the support of his family. We will repay his generosity whatever it takes. I freely admit he has taken a great weight off my shoulders and for that I will be eternally grateful.' She paused. 'I pray Hugh sees it in the same light.'

Ela noted the doubt in the eyes of the speaker.

§

If Isolde de Audley felt relieved, the king of England felt quite the opposite. He sat gazing at the crumpled scroll and the nervous messenger who he was in no doubt how the news had affected his sovereign as a curse roared from the royal lips. In growling tones, the king barked.

'Damn these accursed Scots. Who is this William Wallace?' He glared at the messenger.

'I,.... I do not rightly know, Sire, only that he murdered one of your sheriff's.'

'Is that all you can tell me, dolt?'

The young man blanched at the rebuke.

'Sire, I have brought the message from Lord Cressingham, the original messenger was sore wounded, and therefore, I know naught of the exact details.'

The steel blue eyes raked the figure before him and then nodded.

Edward raised his hand in a gesture of dismissal and the messenger withdrew with all haste. By the date on the message, it had been some weeks since the event had actually taken place. Fate had reined some bitter blows upon the royal head over the past weeks, now this! Angry as he was, Edward's mind quickly assessed the actual sequence of events of this attack on one of his law officers. It had in fact occurred before his brother's death and the defeat of his army in France. He sat fuming for a while then rose, and swept out of the chamber to his own apartments. He called for a cup of wine and as he quaffed the rich liquid, he mulled over the issues that beset him. After much deliberation, he finally came to the decision to lead an army into France and take his revenge on his French enemies. Under his banner, men would fight or die, and no one would desert their royal master without dire consequences. He would rescue de Lacy and his knights and make the French pay dearly for being the cause, however indirectly, of his brother's death. The Scottish matter could be dealt with by Surrey who was one of his most trusted commanders.

After the body of Edmund Plantagenet had been laid to rest in Westminster Abbey, Edward lost no time in raising an army and by the 24th August, he had set sail for France to join his ally, the Flemish Count Guy Dampierre. Among his retinue was Sir Nicolas de Audley. Before he left, Edward had sent word to John de Warenne, the Earl of Surrey, to take charge of his army in Scotland confident that his experienced commander could bring about the downfall of the upstart rebel, William Wallace.

However, against all odds, the rag tag forces of the rebellious William Wallace had achieved a resounding victory at Stirling Bridge on the 11th day of September. Edward was so incensed at the news that he shut himself away for a day and vowed to wipe this defiant Scot from the face of the earth. He had no notion that the name of Wallace would be scorched on his heart for years to come. It mattered little that in fact, the knave who had routed one of his most experienced commanders was not even a true Scot but a Northumbrian lordling.

Over the winter months, Isolde had no news of her husband or her brother-in-law and so wrote to the Lady Katherine to glean some knowledge of events in France. In her reply, Katherine Giffard had written that there had been a treaty signed by Edward and Philip IV of France but no sign of the return of their husbands to England. She knew nothing of Hugh and scant details of Nicolas but took heart that at least they must both be alive. However, there was an invitation for James and Hugh to visit Heileigh Castle, an invitation Isolde saw as an excellent opportunity for her sons to forge closer family ties with their cousins.

If Katherine de Audley had received no news from France this was not the case with Richard FitzAlan, Earl of Arundel, who felt satisfied upon learning that the king had signed the Confirmation of Charters and had finally issued a statute confirming the Magna Carta. He also learned that Edward was to marry the young sister of Philip of France, Marguerite. The Earl also felt vindicated for seeking the annulment of his sister's marriage as Edward had taken all the captured Scots nobles from the English victory at Dunbar to fight for him in France which was part of their conditions of ransom. Such an act would not endear him to them and would undoubtedly harden the proud Scots resolve to seek revenge once they were free.

Meantime, on an icy winter's morning in Pembridge, the bowed figure of the Dowager Lady Mortimer, Maud de Braose, knelt in the church of Saint Mary's, as she listened to the Requiem Mass with a heart heavy with grief. The body of Guy de Longeville was laid to rest with all the quiet dignity Maud deemed his due. It had been like watching part of herself being buried. He had died quite suddenly, just slipping from his horse - dead. Maud had brought his body to Pembridge where she had taken up residence so she could be near his grave. Her once proud spirit, dimmed. She had told no one in her family of her loss; her grief was a personal one as Guy, after all, had only been important to her. Besides, Edmund was in Wales, his wife busy with their growing family and Maud wanted to grieve alone. She felt the years closing in on her and her usual vitality appeared sadly lacking. Nevertheless, Maud felt certain she *would* rise again, there was still much to be done in the affairs of the family. The marriage of her favourite grandson, Roger, was now paramount and she must ensure that he made the most prestigious match possible. As she walked slowly from the graveside of her dead companion she straightened her shoulders and vowed to begin her plans for her grandson's future as soon as she felt strong enough to ride. She knew Guy would understand, he had always been her greatest ally and although he was gone from this earth, his spirit would always be at her side and this thought gave her great comfort in the days that followed.

CHAPTER XII

Stratton 1297

After an uncertain summer and with the days beginning to shorten into autumn, a dishevelled messenger arrived bearing a letter, and as Isolde read it she exclaimed.

'By all the Saints in heaven - our lord will be with us in two days!'

Ela looked up from her needlework. Life would now take on a different pattern with the return of the Lord of Stratton, whether that was cause for celebration or not, would soon become clear. She could not read Isolde's expression or know what the true feelings were of the younger woman towards her husband. Relief at his release from prison was certain but .... what affect would that have had on him? She remembered all too well the uncertain moods he had shown on his return from Scotland; how would this latest series of events have affected him? It would undoubtedly, be a period when Isolde would need her support.

Once the news spread of the imminent return of Lord Hugh, the whole castle and its staff became like a hive of bees hurrying about their duties in an effort to make ready apartments and chambers for his arrival. The kitchens too, made haste with baking, stewing and roasting. Whatever produce they could find, as the larders and stores had been depleted by the king's men earlier that year. The gamekeepers and hunters brought conies and hares, ducks, geese and venison, in fact whatever they could snare or catch. Fishes were netted in the rivers, even though it was strictly out of season. As food was so scarce and time so short the normal rules were, for once, ignored for this special occasion.

When Hugh de Audley rode through the gates of Stratton, Isolde let out a gasp for the man that dismounted and walked towards her, bore scant resemblance to the man that had ridden away the previous year. It took her all of her resolve to hide her inner horror. Gone was the tanned, battle hardened knight in fine armour. In his place was a pudgy, pale faced man with a paunch. His hair looked lank and was cut so short, it was more like that worn by a monk than a nobleman, and also gone was the fine moustache. In fact he wore no facial hair at all.

Gallantly Isolde held out her hands in greeting.

'Welcome home, my lord.'

He did not look directly at her but scanned the waiting group.

'Where are my sons?' His tone was flat and hard.

'They are at Heliegh, my lord.'

'What are they doing there? You should have known I would want to see them on my return and I sent plenty of warning.'

'I assure you my lord, your messenger only arrived two days since.'

'I sent one from France as soon as I was ransomed.'

'Well he must have been waylaid, or worse, killed, as your message never reached here, my lord.'

'Well you can send for them forthwith.'

Isolde liked neither his manner or his tone. Her dark eyes flashed as she replied tartly.

'I will not be spoken to thus, my Lord. I am not your servant.' She turned on her heel, walked back to the doorway and swept passed the waiting servants, her face full of anger. Ela fell in step with her mistress. This did not bode well and she braced herself for the outburst of emotion she knew would follow.

Neither saw the look of outrage on Hugh de Audley's face or heard his bellowed orders to dismiss all the servants. He stumped into the home he had left all those months ago and already felt a pang of regret at speaking to his wife so brusquely. If his messenger had never arrived then it was certainly no fault of Isolde. He beckoned a page who stood in the shadows of the passage.

'There is a leather satchel among my boxes and trunks I wish you to take to your Mistress.'

The page bowed and sped off to do his master's bidding.

Meanwhile, Ela had been correct in her assumption of the actions of her Mistress for as they entered her chamber, Isolde picked up a ewer and threw it at the wall. Ela waited until the moment of fury passed then as she began to gather the broken pieces she said softly.

'I beg you, do not make this incident into an irreconcilable difference. Remember, he has been incarcerated for months and........' She did not finish her sentence as Isolde came and stooping helped to mop up the spilled water.

'I care not. I will not be spoken to thus in front of the servants.' She paused then said in a softer tone. 'You are right. I was too hasty, mayhap he will consider the situation and apologise.'

As she finished speaking a light knock on the door interrupted the two women from their task. Upon opening the door, Isolde saw a small page holding a leather bag.

'Excuse me your Ladyship, Lord Hugh has sent me to give you this ......' he thrust the soft leather bag towards her as he hesitated, 'and asks you to accept it with his regrets if he has offended you.'

Isolde took the proffered bag as the page bowed and stood, awaiting her reply. Her curiosity aroused, Isolde opened the drawstring and let out a gasp.

'Why, I do believe it is a gittern. How do you suppose he came across such an instrument?'

'Well, it matters not where it came from only that he thought of you and brought it to please you.' Ela felt relieved that Isolde's anger had subsided, replaced by delight at the gift. Music had always been one of her pleasures and the unexpected present was something she knew Isolde would treasure. As she disposed of the fragments of pottery, Isolde's fingers were already caressing the strings and the melodic notes filled the chamber. She turned to the page.

'Tell his Lordship his gift has been accepted.'

Sometime later, another knock came but this time it was louder and when Ela opened it, framed in the doorwell was Hugh de Audley. She turned to announce the visitor when Isolde came and stood before her husband. She extended her hands and said in an even tone.

'Shall we start again my Lord? Welcome home.'

Hugh raised her hands to his lips.

'I fear my homecoming was not as either of us would have wished!'

Isolde looked up into his pallid face.

'You have suffered much my Lord and it is therefore best we forget the incident.'

'I do not deserve your understanding but do admit freely that my experiences in France have not improved my temper.' He noted the gittern. 'Does the gift find favour?' He paused. 'Nicolas said it would.'

'You mean it was your brother's idea to buy the gittern for me?'

'Indeed!'

Isolde turned away to hide the expression of her face but Ela had seen the change and crossed her fingers hoping there was no tart comment to follow. However, when Isolde turned back there was a fixed smile on her face.

'A kind thought and I shall have many hours of pleasure perfecting my skills.' Isolde stood back for him to enter and then went and poured him a cup of wine. She felt relieved that she had not flung the jug of wine in her anger. After a pause Isolde looked up, her face full of eagerness. 'We could go to Heleigh and collect the boys together, once you have rested.'

He nodded. 'I like that idea and will write and let my brother know of our intentions.'

There were no further crossed words during the rest of his visit and after his departure Isolde sat for a long time, quite still, her hands folded in her lap, lost in deep thought. Ela knew better than to arouse her, so without fuss called for a servant to take away the broken crockery and used wine cups.

A few days later Lord and Lady de Audley began their journey to Heleigh Castle for a family reunion. Upon their arrival, they were greeted with the youthful exuberance of their two boys, and Hugh, without any preamble said,

'Papa, you have grown fat and what manner of hairstyle is that? You look more like a monk than a knight!'

'Hugh, you should not speak to you father thus. Besides, it is rude to make personal comments.'

Hugh just grinned. 'But it is true Mama!'

James dug his elbows into Hugh's side. 'Hush, you have said too much!'

'But .....'

'Well, fat or not, I am pleased to see how you two have grown, even if my youngest son's manners do not appear to have grown overmuch during my absence.'

A ripple of mirth ran round the group as Lord Nicolas and his wife ushered their guests into the vaulted hall of Heleigh Castle.

'I am afraid the fare will be abstemious as it is still Advent but I insist that you all stay for the Christmastide festivities so we can all relax and spend some precious time as a family.'

The younger members clapped their hands with glee but Hugh senior's face grew serious.

'I should go and see our mother.'

Nicolas smiled. 'There is no need, as I stopped to collect our mother on my homeward journey and she is here, at Heleigh. Sadly she has declined into a state of senility and knows little of what or even where she is. She is being well looked after and therefore we can now spend as much time as possible with our wives and children. Our mother can relax and stay quiet and we can visit her without stressing her too much'

Isolde thought she heard a note of unease in her brother-in-law's words but kept her thoughts to herself.

In the days that followed, the tensions of the previous months slowly began to seep away from the older members of the de Audley family. Isolde noted how her sons James, and Hugh, enjoyed the company of their cousins as they all got along so well, even though Thomas often had to miss some of the rougher games due to his weak chest. She was pleased to see how her eldest son looked after his cousin and Ela the little girl who would one day marry Thomas, Eve Clavering. He was growing up fast and it would not be long before he went to court as one of the king's squires in the following spring.

James was of a more serious nature than that of his brother Hugh. He had not inherited the russet hair or hazel eyes and she noted the likeness he bore to his maternal family, the Mortimers. It was obvious he would grow taller than his father and more handsome. Hugh, on the other hand, was all de Audley in looks, with a far more outgoing and outspoken character; the latter she judged he had inherited from her and a trait she would have to teach him to guard against in future.

Christmas was a joyful occasion and one which each of the family would remember in the years to follow. A time, when Hugh's paunch grew less each day with all the hunting and sword practice, and Isolde and Katherine Giffard, became, if not exactly close, far more at ease with each other than previously. Katherine had a warmer nature than she often portrayed in public.

However, all too soon, the time came for the junior members of the family to take their leave and return to Oxfordshire but the feeling of warmth and well being remained for many days after and they laughed and joked together on their homeward journey.

Sadly, the festive mood quickly wilted with a summons from the king to attend Parliament and Hugh and Isolde made ready for yet another journey but this time southward.

Isolde voiced her apprehensions to Ela as they sorted through her kirtles, cloaks and headdresses.

'I dislike the court. It is a hotbed of gossip and mischief, so often hidden by a fixed smiles and outrageous demonstrations of friendship. I find such hypocrisy galling.'

'Nevertheless, the standing of the Audley family is respected in most quarters and has been for many decades.' Ela said as she briskly brushed a fur hat. 'Especially by the king and that must stand for a great deal.'

'Of course but ....' Isolde tossed a shift across the bed towards the open trunk; 'I find it an unsettling place and feel I fall short of the fashions and courtly ways and affectations expected of courtiers.'

'Well, just watch, listen and promote your family whenever the opportunity arises. That is all you can do – and .....' Ela looked up at Isolde; 'please try and keep out of trouble!'

At that, Isolde chuckled as they continued with their task of packing.

'Methinks I will give such advice to young Hugh when he departs for Windsor.'

Upon their arrival in London, they found their lodgings shabby but comfortable, and Isolde was glad they were not under the same roof as the king's party. Nicolas and Katherine soon joined them but the mood was tense, as all knew the main reasons for the king's summons. For he was not only seeking funds for the next incursion into Scotland but there was also the nagging question of the Forest Charter; another pertinent issue between the sovereign and many landowning magnates. Like the Magna Carta, this contentious issue had been festering since the time of Henry III. There was no doubt the nobles and magnates knew it was their coffers, which would bear the expense of the ambitions of the king in his Scottish wars. Even the voices of his most senior advisors were raised in opposition to the crippling taxes but it appeared to make scant difference. Now the whole matter was becoming more aggressive on both sides especially as a number of landowners, through the decades, had lost considerable amounts of land to the crown in its encroachment of the royal hunting pursuits. Even to the extent that some men had been convicted of poaching on ground, which legally belonged to them.

Each evening as the family dined, the topic was invariably about money, land and Scotland. Hugh's temper would flare like dry tinder before a flame as the realisation came that he would need to borrow yet even more money to fund the men, armour and horses expected by the king.

However, Isolde was to find a more personal subject to send her thoughts into disarray and one, which was quite unexpected. As she walked through the shadowy passages of Westminster, she heard low voices coming from a chamber to her right and recognised one as that of her husband. Pausing, to discover whom he was talking to, she caught the tones of a woman and as she strained to hear more, was stunned at what she heard. The voice was heavily accented and low and breathless but she heard the words .... 'Be careful, mon amour.'

Hugh's voice answered, 'How can I when my blood burns with passion and my body aches to possess you.'

Isolde made a move to the door when Ela's hand caught her sleeve and pulled her back. Without saying a word, Ela indicated for them to leave but Isolde remained rooted to the spot.

Shaking her head Ela continued to pull her Mistress away. When out of earshot Isolde hissed.

'Why!'

'You will drive a permanent wedge between you if you shame him now.'

'You condone .....

'Never, but I do know that a marriage is founded on more than passion and lust. If you are honest, you are not in love your husband but you were raised in the tradition of loyalty and *that* is what is important. Make a scene here, today, and it will be talked of for months casting a shadow over your husband's reputation. Remember, your sons are soon to come to court, do you wish them to be the butt of the gossiper's cruel tongues?'

Isolde took a deep breath: her emotions were in turmoil. 'I cannot deny your wisdom but cannot bring myself to agree.' Inwardly she was seething at this betrayal especially as she was now certain she was pregnant again.

'This is not a time to take personal revenge there are more subtle methods of dealing with this situation. Come – come away now and we will find a better way to deal with this association.'

Hesitantly at first Isolde followed Ela until they reached the doorway. She took a deep gulp of air.

'She is French on that I am certain.'

'Maybe she is one of Lady Blanche's entourage. Besides do you wish to embarrass the king?'

Isolde remained silent as she walked back towards their lodgings but her thoughts were ful, of revenge. Slowly as the two women reached the gardens, Ela guided Isolde to a bench. The cold air had penetrated the consciousness of the younger woman.

'What now? What do *you* propose the next move should be?'

Ela reached over and took Isolde's hands. 'I am unsure but I do know act in haste and you may repent your hasty actions.' After a long pause, Ela said softly, 'I would bring this to the attention of Lord Nicolas, he will know what is best.'

'Mmm! Maybe you are right for I could not trust myself right now not to react more violently towards either Hugh or his French whore.' She looked hard at Ela. 'We must find out the identity of this woman.'

'I think Lord Nicolas will find that out more easily and discreetly than either of us but, if *you* tell him, then your husband may come to see it as an act of spite. Instead, I could mention this liaison to Mabel, Lady Katherine's waiting woman, who no doubt will pass it on, then neither of us can be implicated especially if I make Mabel swear not to reveal her source.'

Isolde nodded. 'How clever you are, Ela. Then whatever actions Lady Katherine takes we can plead ignorance.' She smiled. 'I like this plan and can bide my time on seeking a suitable revenge in future. It will give me the moral high ground and if I have learned nothing else, I have learned that to hold such a position usually ends in victory.'

Ela breathed a sigh of relief. She had averted what could have been a serious breakdown in the marriage of Isolde and Hugh and, at all costs, she did not want her Mistress to spend years of frustration and unhappiness which would have been the outcome had Isolde confronted her husband. There would have been no going back - no path of reconciliation.

After Ela had spoken with Mabel, emphasising her dilemma on what course to take, Mabel assured her that Lady Katherine would know exactly what to do under the circumstances. At the meal that evening, the expressions on the faces of Lord Nicolas and his wife left no one in doubt that something was seriously amiss.

Lord Nicolas indicated the servants not to bring in the food. He turned to his brother and spoke in lowered tones.

'Before we say grace, I would speak with you privately.'

Hugh's expression was full of wariness as he followed his brother from the chamber.

As soon as the two men were alone Nicolas turned on the younger man.

'What is this I hear of you meeting your paramour here, at Westminster, with your wife nearbye? Are you mad?' He began pacing up and down the antechamber, his face full of fury.

'Our father and grandsire served long and loyal service and earned reputation and respect at court and especially with the king; a position you and I have inherited. Are you prepared to lose it all for the sake of lifting a skirt? Besides, the Mortimers are sure to hear of this and will no doubt voice their disapproval in no uncertain terms.'

'This is none of your business.'

'That is where you are wrong. Have you forgotten how much in debt we are already? Some of that is due to the monies raised for your ransom and what of Isolde, she had to live as frugally as possible not to incur further debt. Is this how you repay her?'

'I am all too aware of everyone's sacrifice but it is not uncommon for a man to take a mistress.'

'Discreetly and not where your name can be bandied about and be the butt of sneers and spite. Isolde is no shrinking violet and once she learns she has become a cuckolded wife, I can well imagine how uncomfortable your life will become. Who is the siren that has tempted you away from the path of God?'

Hugh stood looking decidedly uncomfortable, his face a dull red and his expression was that of a scolded child.

'She is the Lady Ankaret Dampierre, a distant relative of the Count. We met in Gascony, before I was taken prisoner and upon my release she...'

'Spare me the details but what is she doing here?'

'She is part of the Count's entourage and she wrote to me upon her arrival in England.'

'You may be playing a very dangerous game little brother for she could be a spy for France.'

'Never, Ankaret would not betray me nor, do I believe she is even sympathetic towards the French king.'

'Do not be so naive Hugh, how often has a pretty face been used to seek out the secrets of a country?'

Hugh's face became sullen.

'I will have your promise that this affair is at an end.'

Hugh shook his head. 'You cannot force me.'

'No, this is true, but let me remind you who it is that stands surety for your debts?'

Without further ado, Nicolas left, but not before urging Hugh to make haste as their wives were waiting.

The atmosphere at the meal was tense and conversation at a minimum. Isolde kept her eyes fixed on the table for the most part, as Lady Katherine made comments on the tenderness of the lamb but the two men remained for the most part, silent. From under her lids, Isolde watched Hugh and could see how uncomfortable he was and she felt a great surge of gratitude towards her brother-in-law for, she guessed he had remonstrated with Hugh about his misconduct. When she was finally alone with Ela, Isolde voiced her thoughts; 'Your plan has worked well in as much as it has discomforted my husband but whether it will bring him to his senses is another matter. Besides, we still do not know the identity of his paramour.'

'You have to give it time. Now he knows his secret is no more he must gauged the consequences without the shroud of secrecy.' She stroked Isolde's back gently. 'Have patience, you will see, Lord Nicolas is a resourceful man and no doubt, will have a plan to thwart his brother's affair.'

Little did either woman know that before Nicolas de Audley had spoken to his brother, the Lady Ankaret had received a message recalling her back to France? The note also stated that if she failed to comply, the life of her lover would be forfeit. The fearful young woman packed and left London that very night. Ankaret sent word to Hugh, with a brief explanation that she had been ordered home by her father and begged his forgiveness, but not to try and contact her or she would be sent to a nunnery.

As Hugh read the words, he cursed and made enquiries to the time of the Lady's departure but learned she would sail on the dawn tide. He knew that even the fastest horse would not get him to the port in time to stop her from leaving the country. Frustrated and angry, Hugh stumped into the council chamber in high dudgeon. As he spied his brother, he glowered at him but remained silent. He little guessed it had been his brother's hand that had written the message to Ankaret.

For her part, Isolde waited a few days then told Hugh she was with child. She hoped the news would prick his conscience further for she knew he felt pangs of guilt. Somehow, it helped to heal the wound she had felt at his betrayal. Glad that Ela's advice had proved wise, she played the innocent in, both, having knowledge of her husband's transgressions and of the move by Nicolas to halt the affair.

The homeward journey was made in easy stages; in part due to the boggy roads but also due to Isolde's pregnancy. Once back in familiar surroundings, Isolde began to relax. She encouraged Hugh to go hunting and in the evenings talk over the plans for the future now that it was certain he would have to serve again in Scotland, as the king was determined to bring the Scots under his heel. Hugh, still ignorant that Isolde knew of his affair, continued to feel guilty, especially on hearing that she was with child. A child conceived in the happy atmosphere of the Christmas festivities, which seemed so long ago now. He felt uneasy at the rift, which had opened between himself and his brother. The harsh words had finally hit their target and it was true – money would be a very difficult issue given the number of men he would have to arm and train in readiness for the forthcoming conflict. He had scant time to grieve for his lost love but in moments of quiet, ached for the sound of her voice and the touch of her skin.

Isolde, sensed the inner struggle of her husband but with great restraint never showed her true feelings of disappointment in him as she wished to make her marriage a sound, strong union, one, which would withstand the weakness of passing passions. As she mulled over these thoughts, her mind travelled back to her own childhood and realised how Lady Maud de Braose must have felt when she had been plunged into the Mortimer household, all those years ago. As she pondered on the memories, she knew that under no circumstances could she raise a bastard, and a new appreciation of her former mentor, the indomitable Lady of Wigmore, grew from that moment.

Meanwhile, as Isolde prepared for the birth of her baby her husband and brother-in-law, heading a company of knights, squires and troops rode out to meet the army of the king.

CHAPTER XIII

July 1298

As Hugh and Nicolas de Audley travelled north, their awkward relationship began to ease, for there were too many pressing matters on that difficult journey than to hold useless grudges. Delays, due to broken wagon wheels, broken harnesses and lamed horses frustrated the progress. Eventually, when they finally arrived in York, it was obvious that many of Edward's troops were mercenaries gathered from Gascony, crossbowmen from France, longbow men from Wales and a number of foot soldiers from Ireland. The heavy cavalry, however, were mainly made up of nobles and magnates from England, Scotland and a few from Wales.

'I see Bigod and de Bohun have already camped.' Nicolas looked round and spied the familiar standards of the Earls of Norfolk and Hereford.

'I hear that Anthony Bek, the esteemed Bishop of Durham is to join our numbers.'

Nicolas chuckled. 'A holy man who obviously enjoys the physicality of '*swords and arrows*' of war, rather than the spiritual one of prayer!' The two brothers grinned at each other as they rode through the encampment.

Within days they were heading into Scotland and on the journey, the king's forces found they were under constant attack from clouds of midges, as well as from night raiders and the grumbles of the men were growing ever louder.

'I swear by all the Saints. I have barely a square inch of flesh that has not been bitten by these accursed insects. A fate also suffered by my horse.' Hugh's voice sounded irritable as he waved his hand around his head in an effort to keep the mosquitoes at bay.

'We are all suffering the same fate so try and keep your temper in check.' Nicolas was also bearing the marks of many bites but tried to concentrate on watching out for any sudden attacks of the human kind. Some of the mules and sumpter horses were kicking out, the former braying their annoyance.

'Try and keep those animals quiet, they announce our whereabouts like heralds.' Nicolas barked his orders to the drivers who muttered curses under their breath but endeavoured to do his bidding. Lord de Audley was not a man to be disobeyed!

'Once we make camp tonight see if anyone can come up with some method of keeping these pesky little buggers away from our animals - they are losing too much condition for my liking.' Nicolas said to one of his grooms.

'Aye my lord I will see what can be done.'

'Good man!'

Nicolas threw off his gauntlets and ran his fingers through his hair.

'It's obvious that Wallace is not going to give us any help from his scorched earth policy.'

'It matters little as we shall be supplied by sea. The king has ensured his troops will not go wanting.' Hugh squatted before the busy fire for the night had grown unexpectedly chilly.

'Not if this westerly wind persists. No ships can land in such conditions. Our horses will soon be in need of fodder for we have found no forage for days and soon we will feel the ache in our own bellies from lack food.'

Hugh grunted. 'Then let the Godly Bishop pray for the wind to change as he has the ear of the Lord!'

'Watch what you say or you may feel the stroke of his mitre on your head.'

They soon left Roxburgh Castle behind and continued on their way toward the Lothian coast but Wallace evaded open battle, as they encountered only skirmishing parties which harried the English army on its journey northwards. The Castle of Direlton was quickly overrun, so they continued towards Linlithgow but the winds still blew hard from the west and the whole army and its horses began to suffer from lack of food.

The situation had become so bad that Edward was on the point of giving the order to withdraw when the long awaited supplies arrived. The mood changed and the king continued north. One late afternoon, a fast riding party headed by Patrick Dunbar, Earl of March, brought vital information as to the whereabouts of the elusive Wallace who some of his scouts had spied camped just seven miles away on the Stirling road. With his enemy so close, Edward mobilised his troops and that night they all slept in battle dress with their horses tethered close, so close in fact that the following morning, it was reported, that the king had suffered broken ribs due to the fact his horse had stepped on him during the night. At dawn on the twenty-second day of July, the English army came in sight of Wallace at the small town of Falkirk, which lay close to an old Roman Fort.

Wallace, faced by his English adversaries, now had little choice but to stand and fight. Although outnumbered, he felt that with the advantage of the better ground and a stream and bog to protect his position, which put his enemies at a disadvantage. It was essential that Stirling Castle should not fall to the English, for it was a vital crossing into Northern Scotland.

As the Scots forces faced their enemy it was obvious that the Edward's forces were by far the more superior army made up of well seasoned troops. The main contingent was a heavy cavalry division, supported by companies of crossbowmen mainly from Gascony and longbow men from Wales and the Welsh Marches. Although the king was in overall charge, he deployed his forces into three divisions the vanguard, which was mainly heavy cavalry, led by Roger Bigod, the Earl of Norfolk, Humphrey de Bohun, the Earl of Hereford and Henry de Lacy, Earl of Lincoln. The central guard was under the command of Anthony Bek, the Bishop of Durham, supported by Ralph Bassett, his deputy, and the rear guard, which was under the direct command of the king.

The Scots, who were drawn up in four, tightly packed schiltrons, with archers positioned between each schiltron, had also erected a palisade of sharpened stakes. The small company of light cavalry was held to the rear. With the advantage of the firm ground, the Scots waited for the English to charge.

The two de Audley brothers sat knee to knee on their restless chargers. A young Irish squire held aloft their bright standard of '*gules vel fretty or*' which fluttered in the morning breeze.

'Hold your line Brendon and don't forge ahead, remember to keep close.'

'Aye my Lord.' The young squire's face was alight with excitement, his mount as anxious as he was to be off.'

'God go with us this day'. Nicolas looked at his brother and their small band of squires.

Then, they heard the hoarse voice of Roger Bigod who ordered the charge. Many of the great warhorses knew the command and plunged forward in line. However, as they surged forward, they were quickly slowed by the soft, boggy ground and the initial impetus was soon dissipated as the chargers became trapped. The bulk of the numbers began to veer to the right. On seeing this the Bishop moved his men steadily to the left which opened up the opportunity for an attack on the flanks of the Scots but, if Bek was wary his deputy, Ralph Bassett, urged his men on regardless of the dangers. When they too, encountered the marshy and boggy ground also slowing them down. Although they could not penetrate the schiltrons, they turned on the Scottish archers, who had been left exposed to attack, as their cavalry had fled the field, leaving their comrades to fight and die under the merciless lances and swords of the English.

As Edward sat and watched the battle, he could see how his cavalry were now becoming more of a pincer movement but he needed them to break the schiltron formations and sounded the recall and once the bulk of the heavy cavalry had joined his ranks, he ordered his archers forward to attack the Scottish schiltrons. The hail of arrows that rained down on the static formations soon began to take heavy casualties and gaps began to appear. On seeing this, the king then ordered the cavalry forward, and, with ruthless efficiency they slaughtered the routed Scots. However, during the debacle, Wallace had escaped, much to the chagrin of Edward, but his reputation as '*Guardian of Scotland*', had been shattered.

Although most of the Scottish army had been slain, there had been some heavy losses to the English infantry and it was some time before the true state of affairs was clear.

Nicolas removed his helm; blood streaming down his face as he went in search of his brother. Brendon had stayed at his side throughout and still proudly held the de Audley colours.

'You did well and I shall write and tell your father of your valour.'

The young squire grinned. Only now did his arm start to shake as he handed the standard to another as he dismounted.

'Go and see if you can find Lord Hugh and afterwards learn if we lost any men and horses.'

'Aye, my Lord.' He paused. 'Are you hurt my Lord?'

'No!' He wiped his face. 'It must be someone else's blood.'

Eventually the brothers were reunited. Hugh was cursing his ill fortune at losing his lance.

'It broke like a twig, fortunately I managed to seize another but it is of inferior quality.'

'The ground could have been our undoing I saw a lot come to grief - stuck in the mud.'

Hugh nodded. 'Thankfully, we were better mounted than some and the strength and courage of our chargers undoubtedly saved our lives as a number foundered in the mire.'

Upon Brendon's return, he learned the heartening news that only a few of the de Audley contingent had been wounded with none had been killed.

'And what of the the horses?'

'Sadly, Miles lost his mount, my Lord, and suffered a dislocated shoulder from his fall but apart from a few cuts and grazes the rest appear alright, so far. Yancy said it would be the morrow that would be the telling time.'

'Then let us hope that our luck holds. Are any of our men seriously wounded?'

'Not unless any of the wounds becomes infected.'

'Good, then we can at least eat our supper and get some much needed rest for I doubt if the king will wish to stay hereabouts for long.'

'He will hunt Wallace like a stag and not be satisfied until he is brought to bay.'

The following morning the order came for the troops to mount up and continue on to Stirling. They took the Castle within two weeks but Edward wasted no time in celebrations and was once more heading northwards but not before he had taken the decision to dismiss his infantry. Only those mounted would continue in the hunt for the traitor, Wallace, but he had added another name to the list, that of Robert de Brus.

Now they headed west into Carrick, the lands of the Brus family. By the time they reached the west coast town of Ayr, Brus had burned his castle and their quarry had once more eluded the English forces.

Incensed that once again, their enemy had thwarted them, Edward now faced further difficulties when his fleet of supply ships failed to materialize. After kicking their heels for a week, the plan to go on to Galloway lay in ruins. The English now changed direction and headed down the coast of Annandale, seizing the Brus Castle at Lochmaben.

However, Edward faced an even more serious matter, one which involved the Earl's of Hereford and Norfolk, which all hinged on the distribution of Scottish lands. In fact, this particular issue had begun during the wars in Wales, when he had distributed lands to his friends, John de Warenne, the Earl of Surrey and Henry de Lacy, the Earl of Lincoln but none to the Earl's of Hereford and Norfolk.

Once again the king was about to ignore his former promises of reward for the efforts of Humphrey de Bohun and Roger Bigod and the matter came to a head when Edward awarded the Isle of Arran to an Irish mercenary, Hugh Bissett but nothing to the Earls in question. By the time the army reached Carlisle, de Bohun and Bigod made their cursory excuses and left to make their way back to England. The mood amid the camp was now one of unease. There were many who agreed with Hereford and Norfolk and part of the grumblings aired by some, was the issue of the Forest Charter, which the king had already promised to address together with those contained in the Magna Carta. If the king had failed to fulfil his promises to the Earls, how did that leave those given on other matters?

The de Audley brothers were caught up in the change of mood of those left in the camp and Nicolas warned his brother to keep quiet as unguarded comments could prove dangerous, not only for now but for the future.

'Nevertheless, it is quite plain that Edward Plantagenet does not forget those that oppose him and Bigod and de Bohun were very vocal in their dissent on the church tax.'

'Then that should tell you everything about our king, I suggest you learn by that observation.' The tone of the older brother held an unmistakable warning.

The two men buckled on their armour in readiness for the next castle to be taken on their route back towards the borders, and that was Jedburgh.

'Does the king believe that a small garrison can withstand a Scottish onslaught after we are gone? If so, methinks he is badly mistaken.' Hugh muttered to Nicolas.

'Then keep your mouth shut and look as amicable as possible or you may find you have been appointed to the post.'

'Hell fire, I would not wish to spend a minute longer in this place than is absolutely necessary.' Hugh needed no more prompting and for once, followed his brother's advice.

Meanwhile, as the English army continued their campaign in Scotland Isolde was making ready to retire to await the birth of her baby. However, with the weather so warm and pleasant, instead of confining herself within the walls of Stratton she would often sit in the arbour out of sight and stitch quite contentedly, accompanied by her ever faithful companion Ela.

Since the news of the English victory at Falkirk had arrived and she knew that both her husband and brother-in-law were safe, Isolde allowed herself to relax and enjoy these private weeks unencumbered by her normal responsibilities. She prayed for a safe delivery but enjoyed the luxury of just being at peace with her surroundings. The bees were busily gathering nectar from the rich smelling lavender at her feet and the perfume of the honeysuckle that wound together with the roses around the arbour filled the air.

'I think this must be what heaven is like!' She murmured.

'It is the contentment from within that is heaven sent.' Ela said softly.

'I hope my husband has put aside his wayward appetites upon his return and that his military success will have appeased his desires.'

'Come now my dear, this is not the time to dwell on such thoughts. You will only distress yourself and that is not good for your unborn child.'

'I know you are right dearest Ela but I sometimes get a glimpse of the marriage I would wish for - only for it to be snatched away again with Hugh's mood swings.'

'He was spoilt by his mother as a boy, by all accounts, and learned selfishness and self aggrandisement. He is not therefore entirely to blame.'

'He has no concept of how his thoughtlessness affects others.' Isolde sighed.

'Be thankful he does not beat you or keep you in close confinement as I have heard others do!'

Isolde looked hard at Ela. 'And do you think I would meekly allow such treatment?'

Ela's face lit up with a smile. 'Of course not but I do believe that his brother, Lord Nicolas keeps an eye out for your welfare as you were his choice for his brother.'

'How do you know that?'

'I overheard Lord Edmund tell his mother.'

'I wonder why he chose me.'

'Maybe he thought you had a strong enough character to withstand his brother's shortcomings. Apparently his first wife was quite intimidated by him and their mother.'

'God rest the poor soul.'

'Now I think we should go in as I am getting a little too hot.'

Two weeks later, Isolde was delivered of a baby girl who had inherited the red gold hair of her father.

CHAPTER XIV

In late November, a dishevelled party arrived at Stratton, fatigue etched into all of their faces. Without any preamble, Isolde ordered tubs of hot scented water, clean dry clothes and after a brief welcome, let them go and bathe before eating.

The many questions she had wished to ask were held in check for it was apparent they were all weary to the bone. Lord Nicolas spoke first.

'You will never know how we have longed for home: cooked food and clean, fresh linen. Is that not so Hugh?'

'Aye! The journey home was one of the most trying and interminable ones I have ever ridden. Roads, which were feet deep in mud in places and rutted by hard frost and snow. A veritable nightmare!' He exclaimed.

There was a murmur of assent by all. They ate, almost in silence, but with great relish. It was obvious that sleep was the next priority. The following morning as Lord Nicolas was arranging to continue his journey homeward, Isolde begged him to stay for a few more days and after much persuasion, he agreed, greatly to her satisfaction. During his stay, she gained the details of the Scottish venture and understood the hardships endured by each one of them. To lighten the mood she had baby Katherine brought down and noted her husband's face as he held his tiny daughter for the first time.

'My wife will be delighted that you named the babe after her.' Nicolas smiled warmly as he spoke. When he took the little girl in his arms, his face was as soft and tender as any woman's.

'Methinks she has stolen your heart, my lord.'

'Of course. It has been a long time since I have been around a babe, especially one as pretty as little Kate. It makes me long to get back home to my own family.'

'Which is only natural but I do think you should take another day or so just to rest.'

'I know your logic is sound but I must get home as soon as possible for with all that has taken place over this summer, I fear the king will be calling a Parliament as soon as he returns and we shall be bound to attend for there are some serious matters that are far from being resolved. Not only regarding the Scottish wars but issues on the Charters.'

'No doubt, de Bohun and Bigod will not let the slight go without some manner of redress.' Hugh spoke thoughtfully.

'What slight?' Isolde's curiosity was aroused.

'The king failed to bestow some of the Scottish lands and estates to the Earls as he had promised, but did to some of the mercenaries that fought with us.'

Nicolas added. 'It was the same in Wales, was it not?'

'So the king has antagonised two of his most successful and wealthy commanders.'

'You have it in a nutshell.' The tone of the elder brother was serious.

Isolde looked at the two men. 'Is that not a bad move, especially as you have stated the unresolved issues concerning the Forest Charter where their voices could override some of the king's ambitions?'

'Your wife has a keen perception of how matters stand.'

'No doubt the two Earls have many sympathisers who could be called on to also oppose the king. What then?'

'Precisely, and that is at the heart of one of the most contentious issues of the time, notwithstanding Edward's obsession with Scotland.'

'Well, I envy you not on your next visit to court, for the pride of the Earls will not easily be appeased and can well see a war of words when next Parliament sits.' Isolde said thoughtfully.

'Just so, my dear Isolde, and your husband must learn to curb his tongue in such a situation.'

Isolde smiled impishly. 'A great strain on his self discipline, I fear.'

Hugh de Audley glowered at his wife but Nicolas clapped him on the shoulder and grinned.

'Oh, come on Hugh, your wife was merely teasing can you not see that?'

Although somewhat reluctantly, Hugh appeared to have been appeased, on this occasion, but Isolde knew he had taken it to heart. Not such a bad thing, if it helped to make him aware of the dangers of a loose tongue. The thought struck her that his son and namesake had some of these traits but the boy was in search of acceptance and to be liked, which certainly was not the case with Hugh senior.

The following day Nicolas de Audley rode through the gates of Stratton on his journey to Staffordshire. Throughout the winter there was much hammering and clanging as the blacksmith and armourers set about mending chain mail and plate, as well as damaged weapons. The smell of singeing and burning pervaded the air.

'I swear this must be as noisy as a battlefield.' Complained Isolde, one morning as the beat of the hammering continued.

'I am sure it is all necessary, for what I can gather, there will be another foray into Scotland, come summer.'

Isolde knew Ela was right and she should accept it all as part of the life of a knight and his household, nevertheless, she still felt irritated.

In early February, the summons arrived, requesting Lord Hugh to attend Parliament the following month. Hugh's mood changed from being preoccupied to one of annoyance.

'Do you fear another invasion into Scotland?' Isolde asked one evening as they dined.

'I suppose it is inevitable, as we know many of the garrisons we left have been overrun and are once more in the hands of the Scots.'

'So! What of the Forest Charter?'

'No doubt the death of de Bohun will leave Bigod the only voice to openly challenge the king's tardiness as he persistently refuses to address the complaints of his nobles.'

'Is this not the same stance his father took on both the Forest Charter and the Magna Carta?'

'Yes, it has come to my knowledge that the king even returned some of the disputed lands in a show of compliance only to seize them back again.' Hugh looked at his wife. 'Many of our friends have been affected by the constant encroachment and loss of lands. I whole heartedly agree with the Earl of Norfolk but Nicolas wishes me to steer a far more cautious path.'

Isolde sat for a moment. She knew how she responded would be of importance.

'He is conscious that it has been through royal patronage that your family has gained wealth and lands, therefore, I believe your brother wishes to avoid any direct confrontation through loyalty. He is aware how volatile this matter is and merely awaits to see if there is an amicable path to an agreement rather than an outright confrontation, which the king could see as treasonous. He tries to protect us all, methinks.'

Hugh studied his wife for a moment. 'You may well be right.'

'If the Forest Charter affected us directly, I think Lord Nicolas would act differently but hesitates before he throws his weight behind anyone for as we know, people change their minds and allegiances all too easily.' Isolde felt pleased that Hugh had listened to her views.

'Amen to that! Now, let us forget the forthcoming acrimony. No doubt, I shall be thrown into and enjoy what is left of my time at home.'

The few short weeks that followed, Hugh and Isolde spent with their sons who would soon be going to Windsor to begin their time as royal squires. In early March, father and sons rode away from Stratton much to the dismay of their wife and mother. There was so much unrest throughout the country: disaffected landowners, disgruntled nobles who were finding themselves in debt to fund a war, which profited but few. Who knew what would transpire once Parliament sat. Isolde felt frustrated that she could do nothing to help her family and turned back to her duties and the care of baby Kate, in an effort to take her mind of her growing concerns.

Some days later, Hugh and Nicolas de Audley, rode into London, their mood sombre for they both knew that the forthcoming Parliament would be full of bitterness and rancour. The king had previously been loath to listen to the landowner's complaints regarding the Forest Charter. If Edward had been under the illusion that the death of Humphrey de Bohun, the Earl of Hereford, would weaken the voice of Roger Bigod, the forthcoming events were to prove quite a shock to the king who was so use to getting his own way in most matters.

It was soon obvious, Edward Plantagenet did not intend to confirm the Forest Charter but the vigorous objections of Roger Bigod shook even the king and with a promise to speak on the matter on the following day, the session ended. However, Edward slipped away during the night to the frustration of his senior Earl, Roger Bigod. It was obvious to the de Audley brothers, that this whole issue could flare up into civil unrest throughout the kingdom and in such circumstances, there would be far more to lose.

The seriousness of the situation eventually became clear to Edward when Bigod rode into London at the head of a thousand horse with the obvious backing of the citizens of London. However, Edward stubbornly refused to negotiate and after a quarrelsome session, he left for Dover with Bigod riding away in high dudgeon to his castle at Chepstow, in Wales.

The two brothers returned to their respective homes full of misgivings as they saw for themselves the unrest that was creeping through the land with voices openly raised against the king in many quarters.

Edward finally realised the growing unrest could no longer be ignored and in a rare volte-face, he sent letters throughout the kingdom announcing that the Forest Charter was to be upheld and in fact, commissioners had already been employed to carry out the perambulation in the autumn, as laid down in the conditions of the Charter. His actions had the desired effect and tempers began to cool.

'You see, Nicolas was right to stay his support and it is the king who has eventually seen reason.' Isolde looked up at her husband as she spoke.

'I have to concede, on this occasion he was right.' He said grudgingly.

'Oh! Come now, your brother has good instincts on most matters and steers a clever course. There are many enemies at court, it would be all too easy to fall foul of royal favour almost by default.'

'It is not your place to lecture me!'

'You are wrong my lord, as your wife and mother of your children, if I see you step into danger, of course it is my duty to make you aware of it. Just because I support your brother in no way detracts from my loyalty to you.'

Hugh, struck by the vehemence of his wife's outburst stopped his confrontational attitude and continued in a more placatory tone.

'You have inherited your father's brusque manners I see!'

'In this case I am glad of it, for reputations can be won and lost by a careless word or act therefore, I stand by my right to speak when I deem fit.'

He suddenly grinned. 'And God take the hindmost!'

Isolde sensed his change of mood and nodded.

In the days that followed, news arrived that the king's fortunes had changed somewhat with a treaty agreed by the French king, Philip IV, Gascony, would once again be returned to English rule. Part of the agreement was to be a marriage between Philip's daughter, Isabella, and the heir to the English throne, Prince Edward, but the most surprising piece of news was that the king himself would marry the French king's sister, Marguerite, that autumn.

If news from France looked promising, an agent from Scotland brought bleak news and one, which disturbed the Lord of Stratton. The Pope, Boniface had ruled Edward had acted illegally in Scotland and now Wallace was in France where he was finding support. However, it was the news regarding the young Robert de Brus, which caused a frown to furrow the brow of Hugh de Audley when he learned that the heir to the earldom of Carrick was now fully behind the Scottish rebellion. Wallace was a guerrilla fighter and skirmisher but not of the Scottish nobility. This news brought a completely new aspect to the wars and one, which was to set a far more disturbing facet to the conflict.

However, during the month of August, the de Audley family received grave tidings, which shocked Isolde and Hugh to their very core: the sudden death of Lord Nicolas, Lord of Heleigh. Brendon, the squire and standard-bearer for Nicolas, who had carried the letter to Stratton, and it, was plain to see by his countenance how distressed he was by the loss of his beloved lord.

'How did this happen?' Hugh's face was grave and his voice low and full of emotion.

'There was an outbreak of the sweating sickness at Heleigh and his lordship sickened and died within a day. Not even the nursing skills of Lady Katherine could save him. His last words were to bring you to Heleigh and that you look to his wife and children, my Lord.'

'I will return with you on the morrow.' Hugh looked at the stricken face of his wife as he spoke. 'I know I can rely on you to take charge and then follow as soon as possible. Now I must write and tell the king.'

CHAPTER XV

Isolde sat before a long mirror as she watched Ela pack her finest garments into three large trunks. Last week she had attended the funeral of her brother-in-law, today she was preparing to go to Canterbury for the wedding of Edward Plantagenet and Marguerite, the young Princess of France.

'It does not sit easily with me to be going to such an event when we are still in mourning.'

Ela stopped her task. 'It is the right thing to do and Lord Nicolas would be the first to point the necessity of your attendance. Lord Hugh is now, if not in title, the senior member of the family and therefore it falls to you both to honour that position.'

'I know you are right Ela but I still feel uncomfortable to be attending festivities at this time.'

'It is after all, a royal command is it not?' Ela's no nonsense comment did not help her mood. Isolde sighed. 'I suppose you are right but when everyone will be wearing their brightest apparel we shall be in mourning shades.'

'You look well in dark colours, they suit your fair complexion'

'My mother would have been overawed by such finery.' Isolde's voice was full of wistfulness.

Ela went and hugged Isolde in a rare moment of outward affection.

'She would have been proud of the fine Lady you have become and do not forget your father. He was a courageous soldier, trusted and respected by the king so, remember when you are midst the noble throng, you are their equal.'

'Ela, you really do give me such confidence and sound advice. What would I do without you?'

'I dare swear you would manage right well, you are, and always have been, an independent spirit and possess the strength and courage of both your parents. Now let's stop gossiping and allow me finish this packing.'

Two days later Lord and Lady de Audley, with their retinue, left Stratton for the long ride to Canterbury. The closer they got, the busier the roads became.

'It looks like the whole country is coming to see the new Queen!' exclaimed Hugh.

Isolde nodded but could not help wondering what the young French girl was really feeling at the thought of marrying a man older than her father. Isolde's thoughts travelled back to her own youth when she was faced with the same dilemma. Eventually they arrived at their lodgings, glad to be out of the clamouring crowds.

Hugh was to be among the royal attendants who would accompany the king to church. Thus, leaving Isolde and Brendon, who had recently joined their household, to find a place to view the ceremony. The squire had gained an excellent vantage point and was keeping Isolde from being crushed, his broad shoulders acting as a human barrier against the thrusting throng.

'Keep close to me, my Lady, there is a place over there that is less congested.'

As they reached the spot, Isolde let out a sigh of relief.

'Thank you Brendon, I do not know what I would have done without you!'

He grinned. 'Lord Nicolas charged me with looking after you before he died. He knew of his brother's precarious temper.'

Even at the point of death, Nicolas had entrusted her well-being to a loyal squire and the revelation brought a tear to her eye. However, there was little time to dwell on such thoughts as the royal procession had stopped before the mighty door of the Cathedral and the solemn ceremony began. Isolde could see the apprehension on the face of the handsome Princess of France but she spoke her vows in a clear, steady voice.

After the exchange of vows, the king raised the hand of his wife to his lips, turned to the crowd and said; 'Behold your Queen.' Cheering broke out and the throng went wild with delight. So began a week of festivities. On the morrow, there was to be a tournament where many of the knights who hailed from both side of the Channel would participate. As the royal couple led the parade, Isolde noticed her husband was riding beside one of the Queen's ladies-in-waiting and the warm looks, which passed between them left her in no doubt that here was her rival. She could not deny the girl was beautiful. She had long, golden hair, bedecked with jewels, which glittered in the autumn sunlight. Her eyes were blue and round and she had a fulsome figure. Isolde felt a quiver of rage run through her slight frame. If the couple thought she would meekly stand aside and allow this relationship to continue then they were both in for a surprise.

'Brendon, I want you to find out the name of the French woman riding beside his lordship.'

'That is the Lady Ankaret Dampierre, my Lady.' He had caught the venom in her tone.

'I want you to watch if my husband and the Lady meet alone and to inform me immediately.'

Brendon knew by the look in Isolde's eyes that to refuse would bring down her wrath on his head and as he had vowed to serve her, felt no conflict of loyalty towards Lord Hugh. In fact, he was the one who would be breaking the vows of matrimony and committing a mortal sin.

When Isolde reached their lodgings and recounted the whole day's events, Ela was in no doubt that this time Isolde would not heed any words of caution and if she were honest, she did not blame her. As she laid out the kirtle and mantle for the evening feast, she tried to instil a measure of calm and although Isolde struggled not to show her anger, the tension in her back betrayed her true feelings.

Eventually, when she joined her husband to make their way to the venue Isolde spoke but little and Hugh, lost in his own world scarcely appeared to notice. Upon their arrival, the couple were ushered to their places at the royal table. Sometime later, when all were in their seats, the king and his bride entered and all rose, cheered and raised their cups in a toast to the royal couple. Edward stopped before Hugh and Isolde.

'It was a sad day when our dear friend Lord Nicolas died. We both thank you for coming to celebrate our happy occasion when your hearts must be full of sorrow. I lost a faithful friend and he will be in our prayers.' His startling blue gaze travelled over them resting on Isolde then he bowed his head and passed on. Marguerite smiled shyly at Isolde and held her hand for Hugh to kiss, and moved to join her husband at the head of the long table.

The evening seemed interminable to Isolde, she felt estranged from the joyful atmosphere, and as her husband was busy talking avidly to those around them she felt isolated. She noted the portly figure of Henry de Lacy, Earl of Lincoln. At his side was his wife Margaret, sister to Hugh's mother, Ela Longespé. Sitting next to the king was the elderly Earl of Surrey, John de Warenne but there were young faces too. Some had recently inherited their family titles such as Aymer de Valence, Humphrey de Bohun, the young Earl of Hereford and Thomas Plantagenet, now Earl of Lancaster and the king's nephew. Beside him sat his wife, Alice de Lacy, daughter of the Earl of Lincoln thus making Thomas Plantagenet, heir to Lincoln's great wealth, as de Lacy had no surviving sons.

As she gazed round the table a familiar face looked back and smiled, it was Maudie sitting beside her brother, Richard FitzAlan, Earl of Arundel. Isolde smiled back relieved that she would be able to seek out her kinswoman once the feast had finished. Throughout the sumptuous meal, Isolde continued to study the faces of the noble families. Beside the young Queen, sat her step- son, Edward Prince of Wales and beside him was a handsome, dark haired youth, bedecked in expensive and colourful apparel. Any stranger to the gathering would have assumed that he was the prince and only the Plantagenet colouring denoted the true royal prince.

It was with some relief when the feasting had finally finished the king ordered the trestle tables to be moved, in readiness for the performances of the minstrels and mummers. As everyone began to mingle, Maudie came and kissed Isolde's cheeks in greeting.

'I offer my profound condolences, Nicolas was a man of great integrity and his voice of reason will be sorely missed.'

'Indeed, I shall also miss his friendship, he was the only one to curb many of Hugh's more outspoken outbursts. Let us hope that his role as head of the family may prove the brake to his unconsidered actions. Changing the subject, who is that flamboyant figure next to the young Prince?'

Maudie smiled. 'Oh! You mean Piers Gaveston! Have a care, for beautiful he may look but has a tongue as sharp as a Toledo blade. He is the Prince's companion and gives himself too many airs and graces for the likes of most earls and nobles.'

Isolde was intrigued. 'Why so?'

Maudie moved to whisper in her ear. 'He gives all the high and mighty nicknames which fill them full of fury.' She whispered. 'The Earl of Lincoln, is *Burst Belly*, whilst Aymer de Valence has been dubbed, *'Joseph the Jew.'*

Isolde smiled. 'I can well see why such men would take exception to those irreverent titles.'

'The thing is they can do scant to quell his outrageous behaviour because, young as he still is his skills do not lie merely in his words but with sword and lance and he has already downed a number foolhardy enough to challenge him.'

'Will he be among the contestants on the morrow?'

'As yet I am unsure I have not seen the roll call but no doubt Richard will know.'

'Pray do not disturb him on my account, all will be revealed in due course.'

'Let us forget the scandals at court and tell me how you are?' Maudie looked hard at Isolde.

'Do I detect something other than grief and curiosity in those dark eyes?'

Isolde hesitated for a moment then, began to tell Maudie of her doubts regarding her husband's fidelity. 'I know I am not alone and many experience similar relationships but......'

'You are a Mortimer and what is yours is yours alone!'

'It sounds so melodramatic when you put it like that but I do hold loyalty amongst the highest of the virtues.'

'No doubt it was instilled in you at Wigmore, by my beloved grand-dam.' There was pride in Maudie's statement. Before she could say more Piers Gaveston came to join them. He bowed gracefully before speaking.

'Ah! Lady Burnell, will you not introduce me to your charming friend?'

His voice was low and pleasing on the ear.

'This is Lady Isolde Mortimer, the Lady de Audley of Stratton. Be kind Piers, as the Lady Isolde is in mourning for her brother-in-law, Lord Nicolas of Heleigh.'

'I was truly sorry to learn of his death. He was always most civil and kind to me, especially when I first arrived in England. In fact, he taught me to hold my lance correctly, something I shall always be grateful for!' His smile was warm and Isolde thought he was the most handsome creature she had ever seen. She held out her hand and he took it and held it to his lips without actually kissing it.

'Your father was the late Sir Roger Mortimer of Wigmore, a great soldier, was he not?'

Without any hint of embarrassment, Isolde answered clearly.

'Yes, a great Marcher Lord. I am proud to be his bastard daughter.'

'Bravo, bastard blood is as potent as any born the right side of the blanket. I see you have inherited his courage and courage, is something I admire greatly, my Lady. If I can ever be of service, do not hesitate to call on me.' With that, he bowed again and left as swiftly as he had arrived.

'Well – I have never heard Piers Gaveston offer anyone his services so you must have made quite an impression.' Maudie's voice was full of admiration. The rest of the evening passed without any further incident.

The following day was dull but there was a great clamour as the arena was made ready for the afternoon's events. Isolde was busily getting dressed in her finery with Ela fussing over the accessories when a knock came at the door. Ela moved to open it and saw Brendon with a look of embarrassment spread across his handsome features.

'I would speak with the Lady Isolde on a delicate matter.'

Ela beckoned him in and left before closing the door.

'Well! As you wish to see me in private, I suspect you have news on my husband!'

'Indeed my Lady and I feel I have failed you for, when his Lordship went missing from the party, I was about to follow him but was waylaid by someone from back home. He kept me talking, so I could not say for certain where

Lord Hugh went and of course, the Lady Ankaret left with the King and Queen.'

'No mind! I know my husband did not return home until the early hours of this morning so we can assume that he was with the French woman. Continue to keep watch but say nothing to anyone else.'

'You can be assured I will endeavour to be more successful next time.'

'Now, hurry along as I am sure Lord Hugh will be looking for you.'

With a perfunctory bow, Brendon left, passing Ela as she returned.

'Did he confirm your suspicions?'

'Not really Ela, although I think it is pretty conclusive that both went missing around the same time.'

'Well, there is nothing to be done right now other than to finish dressing for the tournament.'

Isolde, seated in the periphery of the royal box watched the spectacle of the cavalcade before the bouts began. Trumpets blared and the brightly coloured banners brightened the dull day. Crowds cheered as the great destriers, in their ornate caparisons danced and sidled as the knights waved to their supporters, their harnesses jingled, as they pranced by.

'I see your husband is not fighting today!' Piers Gaveston spoke without looking at Isolde, his eyes fastened on the scene before them.

'The king wished him to lead the cavalcade and be one of the judges on this occasion.'

'Ah! Then who is riding under the de Audley standard?'

'Brendon of Waterford, he bore the standard for Lord Nicolas at Falkirk.'

'Then he deserves his place. Have you made a wager?'

'I.....never thought to!' Isolde stammered.

'Then allow me!' Piers beckoned a page and handed him some coins, a broad smile on his handsome face.

'It adds a little more excitement to the day. Let us hope you are lucky.'

Maudie joined them. 'Oh! I love a joust, I always think it is far more entertaining than a melee where you often lose sight of the fight.'

Isolde felt a pang of sadness. Lord Nicolas would have excelled at such an occasion but she knew that Brendon would not let them down, as proved later that day, when the tournament trophy was awarded to the triumphant young knight from Ireland. Isolde too, found her purse heavier as she left the arena.

'Well – it has been a day to remember. You are richer, as is Brendon, plus his reputation is enhanced by his efforts and therefore the de Audley family has a new hero. Also, we beat the French. What more could we ask for?' Maudie was euphoric, 'And on the morrow, the hunt - where I can shake the dust off my boots and join in the fun.'

Isolde smiled. Maudie's enthusiasm for life never dimmed and it reminded her of her namesake, Lady Maude de Braose. The evening brought feasting and frivolity and dancing and when Piers Gaveston invited Isolde to step a measure on the floor she hesitated but just for a moment. If Maudie enjoyed hunting and riding, Isolde's forte was music and dancing and as the couple moved gracefully around the floor it was obvious to the onlookers that here was a rare sight, two dancers in perfect harmony and their delight was there for all to see.

'My Lady Isolde, I had no idea you were so talented, you feel every beat of the music.' Gaveston smiled down at his partner.

'We are not all clod hopping peasants from the Shires, my Lord Gaveston.' She quipped but with an impish smile.

The couple were oblivious to the expression of fury on the face of Hugh de Audley as they danced past him. When the dance ended Piers bowed, as Isolde made a low curtsey and left the floor to applause, much to Isolde's embarrassment.

'You looked so elegant out there, a perfect foil for each other, Piers in his multi coloured apparel and you in the dark velvet gown. You will have set the tongues a wagging I'll warrant.'

Before Isolde could respond, her husband stormed over.

'Madam, I wish to speak to you in private.' With that, he turned on his heel and walked briskly towards the exit.

'Oops! Methinks Lord Hugh is somewhat put about by your newfound fame.'

Isolde whispered. 'If he thinks to berate me he will find I have my own weapons with which to defend myself.' She moved swiftly in pursuit of her irate husband. Almost before Isolde had closed the door behind her Hugh turned to face her, his own features as red as his hair in the rush light.

'Exactly what do you think that performance conveyed to everyone?'

'That I am eminently superior at dancing than most of the high born ladies of the court!' Isolde's dark eyes had narrowed in warning.

'Are you aware that Gaveston is despised by all but a handful of nobles?' Isolde noted how beads of sweat quivered on his brow like tiny diamonds.

'Pray, what would you have me do – refuse to dance with one of the king's party? Surely, that would have provoked anger on all sides. Besides, you are not blameless in the matter of propriety, your eyes never left the Lady Dampierre throughout the meal, do you think I and everyone else is blind?'

Hugh made a step closer, his hand raised when a figure from the shadows stepped forward.

'My Lord de Audley, if you wish to strike someone then let it be someone closer to your own size and gender.' Gaveston's voice was low but full of menace, his hand hovered over the jewelled dagger at his belt.

'My Lords, I beg you both to stop! I do not believe my husband was about to strike me.'

Isolde looked hard at Hugh as she spoke. 'I thank you my Lord Gaveston for defending me and hope you will forget this silly episode. Methinks the wine is stronger than we are used to. Is that not the case my Lord?' She stared at Hugh as she spoke. For an instance, she thought he would not take her lead but she saw him draw a deep breath and then nod.

'You are right my Lady, I over reacted.'

'I am sure Lord Gaveston will overlook your rash actions if not for his own sake then for mine.'

'As you wish my Lady Isolde but ....' he turned to de Audley, 'should you wish to take this further I am at your service.'

'However..' he looked hard at Hugh, 'should I ever learn that you have been anything but respectful to Lady Isolde, then you can look to me to avenge her.' He bent and kissed Isolde's hand then left.

'That could have ended badly my Lord,' murmured Isolde.

Hugh grunted, turned on his heel and returned to the festivities. She stood for a moment to gather her wits when she realised she was not alone, another figure stood in the gloom.

'Who is there?'

'Fear not my Lady, it is only me.' Brendon moved into the circle of light. 'I could not openly challenge my Lord Hugh myself, for in so doing, I would have had to leave your service, so I told Lord Gaveston.'

'I am obliged, but it has certainly caused a rift between the Gascon and my husband.

Moreover, who knows what mischief may arise from it. Nonetheless, it gives me comfort to have you care for my well being.' She reached up and kissed his cheek and she left without realizing what emotions had been aroused in the young Irish knight.

Isolde recounted the whole episode to Ela.

'I fear the relationship between my husband and I will never be the same again. However, I do not regret it, things are in the open now and neither of us need pretend anymore. In truth, I shall be glad to return home.'

'Sources tell me the king is hell bent on continuing his war in Scotland. It will be interesting to see if the French king still upholds his position on Scotland now that Edward is his brother-in-law.'

'No matter, wars, marriages, affairs, can all wait until the morrow, for I am tired and will seek my bed.' Isolde stretched and began to undress. 'I do not think we shall see his lordship tonight he will be too busy salving his injured pride in the arms of Mademoiselle Dampierre.'

CHAPTER XVI

Late Sept 1299

The journey from Canterbury was an onerous one, Isolde and Ela rode in the carriage and Lord Hugh led the party. It was obvious, by his stiff back, and lack of conversation with his attendants the state of his mood. When Ela commented on it, Isolde merely shook her head.

'If he wishes to remain aloof then at least we do not have to listen to his words of scorn.' Ela's tone was low so only Isolde could hear.

'No doubt, my husband is not well pleased with the king who has ordered the nobles to muster at York in November. It will not have done anything to help matters.'

The two women continued their journey before Isolde broke the silence. Her word were low and thoughtful.

'The war in Scotland is one which will rage for some time, especially now that Brus and Comyn are vying for the leadership. Baliol was more of a scholar than a soldier, however, from the fragments of conversations I overheard during the celebrations, Comyn is another redheaded hot head and both kinsman and supporter of Baliol, so there is conflict betwixt the two Houses.

Of course, on the release of Baliol last July, it makes matters worse, especially as he is now on the Continent.' Isolde fell silent as the two women mulled over the future and how events across the border would, once again affect their lives. More taxes, more conscription of men and horses, more grain and meat from the larders of the rich for the king's cause.

Finally, they reached Stratton where Isolde found herself faced with a situation, which would once more throw her into open conflict with her husband. Master Linus was the one to outline the situation that one of the tenant's was unable to pay the rent due to murrain in his cattle. The condition was not unknown in the land and it was thought locally, the disease had arrived in the area through a drover diverting his cattle close to the farm in question.

'Master Linus, pray do not bring this information to my husband for I wish to try and resolve the matter myself. The Wood family have been exemplary tenants until this time.'

'There is another matter concerning our own grain, my Lady. They have found ergots in the crop.'

'Damn, damn, damn! This could not come at a worse time, every penny will be required for the forthcoming foray into Scotland and I can well imagine my husband throwing this family out without any recourse. They are good people and ones I trust and therefore, will do all I can to ensure they remain on the land.

'God forbid! It appears that the Fates conspire to thwart our very existence.

'Tell Master Wood I will call on him on the morrow.'

'As you wish, my Lady.' Master Linus was glad that his mistress had taken the matter in hand. Silas Wood and his wife Sarah were God fearing and honest folk and Lady Isolde realised their worth, whereas his lordship had little empathy with any of his tenants. Her steward bowed and left.

The following day was wet and windy but Isolde rode the short distance to the Wood farm ensuring that her husband was busy elsewhere. As she dismounted and handed the reins to her groom, Yancy, she walked slowly up to the door noting the neat garden and cleanliness of the fold yard. The family stood round the large, well scrubbed table as she entered and all bowed or curtseyed.

'Master Wood, I know of your predicament and will intercede with my husband on your behalf. I know how hard you all work and how devastated you all must feel. How many years have your family farmed this land?'

Silas Wood answered nervously. 'Nigh on a hundred years, your ladyship.'

'How long do you think it will take to recover from the loss of your cattle?'

'My wife's father is willing to let us have a couple of his cows but it will take a few years in truth, my Lady.'

Isolde looked at the family; three boys and two girls, all watching her, fear and anxiety in their expressions.

'Say nothing to anyone on this matter, my husband has to recruit and arm men for the wars in Scotland and must be in York by the twelfth of November, therefore his temper is somewhat short these days and to win his approval I must make your case when I deem the moment is right.'

Sarah Wood stepped forward and curtseyed low before Isolde.

'God Bless you my Lady, if there is aught we can do to help you in the future you can rely on us whatever the outcome of his lordship's decision. Is that not so husband?'

'Aye!'

'Then pray I can find the right words and I will send word as soon as I know a decision.'

Isolde's smile was full of sympathy and as she mounted her palfrey, could well imagine the dilemma in which this family now found themselves. She knew her task was going to be difficult, especially in the light of the coolness between herself and her husband. However, even she was surprised at the scene which followed her plea.

'I am not a charitable body and if the family is unable to meet their financial obligations, then they must bear the consequences.'

Isolde stood almost speechless at the vehemence of his statement.

'My Lord, I urge you to reconsider. This is an honest, God fearing family who is well respected in the area, their ancestors have lived here for over a century. Remember, when you are away these are the people on whom I rely to help in emergencies on the farm. Besides, it will create ill will at a time when we need to work together to overcome these hard times.'

Hugh de Audley stared at his wife, it was plain her words had been ignored.

'I have made my decision and that should be enough for you. As my wife it is your duty .....

Isolde felt her anger rise.

'My duty is to ensure that your lands and estates are run with the maximum efficiency. Whilst you are away at war or at court, who do you think oversees the day-to-day business? Me, with the help of Master Linus. The goodwill of the people is essential to enable me to do that and that is how I fulfil *my* duty.' Without further ado, she pulled off her rings, snatched the row of pearls from around her neck and threw them onto the desk breaking the fine chain. The pale beads bounced onto the desk and floor.

'There, that is more than enough to pay for the annual rental of the Wood Farm.' With that, she flounced out her head held high.

The Lord of Stratton sat looking down at the jewels. He was about to follow Isolde when Brendon entered.

'My Lord, I think you should come to the armoury.'

Hugh glared. 'Why?'

'Your suit of armour has gone missing.'

'What?' The word was almost a bark but Brendon knew that he had diverted the rage of his lord from Isolde to this new problem. The sound of the couple's argument had echoed down the corridors and Brendon had acted swiftly in the defence of his mistress. He had hissed the order to Miles to hide Lord de Audley's suit of armour, then entered the study.

Meanwhile, Isolde had returned to her own apartments still in a fury.

'The man is an idiot! He has no notion of sympathy or compassion.'

Ela went and poured a cup of wine and handed it to Isolde as she recounted the scene she had just left.

'Do you think his lordship will accept the jewels?'

'His interest is in material things therefore, I see no reason why not! However, I will happily pawn them, for the Wood family are more important to me than those trinkets.'

Ela felt heartened to hear that Isolde had finally realised that people mattered and that her existence depended on others.

'Well, by all accounts it will only be days before his lordship and the men leave for York.'

'Thank heaven! Although I admit I wish him no physical harm and will pray they all return safely.' Isolde had begun to calm down. 'Why is the man so pig headed?'

Ela smiled. 'I well remember when you were a child you frequently let your temper get the better of you. Admittedly, adulthood and the responsibilities of motherhood have helped to dispel your childish ways. I always knew you had the makings of a strong woman but prayed you would lose the temper and for the most part, that is now the case.'

The days that followed were busy making ready for the imminent departure north and Isolde and Hugh spoke to each other only when necessary. The final evening, Isolde had prepared a feast where all were gathered and only the best food and wine were served. Toasts were made and good wishes exchanged. Prayers were said for the safe return of all and a cheer went up for the Lady of Stratton. Isolde played her gittern and sang songs of heroic tales to the delight of those gathered. Finally, she made a toast to her husband and his squires and all roared their approval. Then she left the gathering to continue with their revelries.

Upon reaching her own apartments, Isolde let out a deep sigh, and as she was about to enter saw Brandon, standing a little way down the passageway.

'You startled me!'

'Forgive me my Lady, I just wished to make my goodbyes in private.'

'Have a care, your actions could be misconstrued and both our reputations come under attack.'

'I merely wanted to assure you I will do all in my power to serve his lordship faithfully and know you are in my thoughts always.'

'Say no more, my lord Brandon. I am conscious of your loyalty and will pray for you all whilst you are away. Now you must go before anyone sees us or misses you from the Hall.'

She did not wait for his response but opened the door and swiftly entered closing it with a loud bang.

'My, what imps of hell are on your tail?' Ela looked at Isolde, who stood still her hand clutching her throat.

'Nothing, I'm sorry!'

'Come, something must have frightened you by the look on your face.'

'Ela, do you think that young Brendon is infatuated with me?'

'Maybe, but then that is part of the culture of knighthood, is it not? Young knight's fighting for the honour of their Lady. You represent.....'

'No! You misunderstand Ela, I think it is more than infatuation I believe he feels he is really in love with me!'

'Come now, he is fulfilling the wishes of Lord Nicolas whom he idolised, that is all. Pray do not fret and try to get some sleep. As it is the last night Lord Hugh may pay you a visit.'

Isolde was not reassured but let Ela start undressing her in readiness for bed.

Hugh did not visit his wife and left at first light the following morning. Many in the retinue were feeling the effects of the wine consumed the previous evening so rode in virtual silence. Hugh did not look back and rode at the head of the column, his back straight and stiff. As the party rode further north, they gauged the atmosphere of the country and whereas in previous marches, men had joined with groups of knights thus swelling their numbers on this occasion, hardly any came to volunteer and the mood of the people appeared somewhat hostile.

This was confirmed when Hugh and his party stayed overnight with a northern Lord Stapleton

'I thought you would have men armed and ready to join us, my Lord'

'You will find precious few from these parts who will answer Edward Plantagenet's call to arms this time.'

'Why so?' Hugh's voice was full of curiosity.

'When the king decides to fulfil his promises to adhere to the laws of the Forest Charter, which, if you recall, he said in early autumn that commissioners had already been recruited to carry out the perambulations, well - to date, there has been no sign of them and not a single acre has been returned to its rightful owners. How can he expect us to fund his wars when he cannot uphold either the Forest Charter or the Magna Carta. It was the same with his father, they just cannot concede that until he respects our rights he can expect no support for his wars. Besides, we have to live with the aftermath of the wars in Scotland. Ask any of my neighbours who have lost cattle, sheep and horses, besides men killed just tending their stock.

No! Edward will have to bend his stiff neck and recognise our rights before we risk our lives.'

'You appear to be well informed, my Lord.'

'Aye, in this matter we have to be as one or all is lost. None wants civil unrest but as king, Edward needs to understand riding roughshod over his barons and landowners will make his position as ruler a very uncomfortable one. Remember, he has already fought in a civil war and reaped the long lasting consequences. Methinks, he will have to reassess his position when he realises his army will only be made up of his Earl's followers and *they* will not be nearly enough to win Scotland.'

Hugh sat mulling over his host's words but remembered advice given by his dead brother, do not speak rashly and on this occasion, he followed the advice and changed the subject to one of family matters.

On the morrow, Hugh and his party left with the good wishes of his host but with a feeling of misgiving that the forthcoming conflict would not be fought with the numbers of troops the king had anticipated, and all knew how this would affect the king's temper. Now, not only were they battling the elements but also deep feelings of doubt that a winter campaign was an ill advised move but also, if Lord Stapleton had been correct in his predictions, then the army would be thinly stretched and that may lead to disaster.

When the de Audley party arrived at York, it was immediately obvious that the infantry was far short of the sixteen thousand Edward had envisaged. In fact, they numbered less than two thousand five hundred. Everything that Lord Stapleton had predicted regarding landowners, barons, and knights, had been correct, it *was* only the knights and retainers of the Earls that made up the majority of the English army. As predicted,

Edward's temper was like a volcano and even his closest advisors and friends were careful how they approached him.

However, for Hugh, he received news which caused him great grief. Isolde had written to tell him of the death of his beloved mother, Ela Longespee. His mood matched that of his sovereign, for he knew that he would be unable to return home in time for her funeral. There was some brighter news, which heartened the king, Stirling Castle had withstood the yearlong siege and he left for Berwick in a better mood.

On their arrival at Berwick, Hugh learned the Queen would be arriving to spend Christmastide with the king and his spirits rose at the thought that Lady Ankaret might be accompanying her. If the news excited Hugh, for his Irish squire, Brandon, it was quite the opposite. He felt uncomfortable, for how could he put an end to this illicit relationship without showing his hand which would subsequently lead to him being banished back to Ireland, thus betraying the solemn vow made to his dead patron. Brandon spent an unhappy Christmas whereas Hugh was elated at being reunited with his pretty French Mistress.

The king, however, had to rethink his strategy for the future and decided to call a Parliament for the following March with the view to readdressing his position regarding the Forest Charter. Men from every walk of life, would be summoned. From, Archbishop Winchelsea to a tonsured friar, burgesses, landowners, barons, lords and knights and men from every shire Edward had finally realised that to achieve one ambition would result in 'tempering' his personal stance on the Forest Charter . His mood of optimism quickly vanished as on his journey back south he learned that Stirling Castle had finally fallen to the Scots.

When Hugh made his farewells to his beloved Ankaret, Brendon breathed a sigh of relief, if Hugh felt no shame for his affair, his squire on the other hand, experienced a sense of failure in his duty to the Lady Isolde and his usual affable nature deserted him on the difficult journey home.

CHAPTER XVII

Early 1300

If the de Audley party hoped the roads would get better the
further they rode south, they were badly mistaken. Snow, ice
and bitter winds swept across the land and when they finally
arrived at Stratton, they and their mounts were exhausted.
With so little notice of their arrival, Isolde and the household
hurried to boil pans of hot water and prepare enough food to
satisfy the returning men. Hugh handed his snow-covered cloak
to a servant who hastened away to brush and dry the heavy
garment. He called for his body servant to assist with his boots
and kicked them off with relief. Isolde came to the hallway.

'Welcome, there is hot water in your chamber. I am sure you
will feel warmer once you have bathed and changed.'

'I began to believe that we would never make it home. The
whole expedition was a complete waste of time.' He moved to
take his wife's proffered hand and kissed it in greeting.

'Well, you are safe now but do not stand too long in those
wet clothes or you will take a chill.'

Hugh gave a wry smile, it was good to be home. Isolde
noticed Brendon and Miles who were waiting for their lord
to dismiss them so they too could go and seek a hot bath and
warm, dry garments.

'I believe you have all lost weight since you were last here.
Scotland does not treat the men of Stratton very well methinks.'
Isolde moved towards them in greeting and the two squires
dutifully bowed and kissed her hands.

'Now quickly go and get warm'. On this occasion, Hugh
was happy to submit to his wife's orders and the three left the
hallway to seek their chambers.

Later that evening as they ate a tasty meal, the conversation turned to events in Scotland and Isolde noted Brendon was unusually quiet, especially when there was mention of the Queen spending Christmastide with her husband at Berwick. By his demeanour, she gathered that the Lady Dampierre had been one of the young Queen's attendants, and therefore, had resumed the adulterous relationship with her husband. Although the news was somewhat surprising, Isolde kept her personal feelings well hidden from the company, only Ela noting a slight change in her composure. When Isolde retired, she made no comment and undressed in silence.

'Has his Lordship said he would be joining you?'

'No! He is too tired.'

Ela looked across as she folded the velvet kirtle.

'Does that please or displease you?'

'I care neither one way nor the other. No doubt you heard of the Queen's visit, so I assume my husband spent the festive season enjoying the charms of his young French whore.'

'Whereas, you spent Christmastide with your sons!'

Isolde smiled, the memory quelled the venom she had felt towards her husband and his paramour.

'I suppose I cannot blame him being attracted to a young, pretty wench but in all honesty. the feeling of betrayal is still a raw wound. Do you think it will ever get better?'

'Time is the greatest healer my dear, concentrate on Kate and your sons and do not dwell on your husband's shortcomings. Men are weak where a comely woman is concerned, my advice, just accept and pay little heed and in that way, you will overcome your jealousy. Besides, he will tire of her no doubt.'

'In truth, I feel no jealousy, for he has never truly loved me or I him but it was always my hope we could find a mutual bond of respect and amity. A vain hope I fear! My feelings towards him are of disappointment at his betrayal, especially as the vow was made before God.'

'Come and seek your bed and put aside such thoughts or you will have nightmares.'

'You are ever my comforter, dearest Ela.'

In the weeks that followed, Hugh had scant time to idle. He was busy looking into his finances where he faced the unenviable truth that his debts were mounting. War was an expensive outlay and even his sons were growing so quickly and needing new clothes and boots. His mood did not improve with the thought of the forthcoming Parliament which he knew would be an acrimonious affair. Edward Plantagenet was stubborn, vindictive and utterly ruthless, so the matter of the Forest Charter and the lack of support in Scotland would not make for easy negotiations. Hugh sighed, if only Nicolas were here with his sound good sense, which he so sorely missed during these difficult times.

As the day drew nearer for Hugh's visit to London, the weather relaxed its icy grip. With but a few retainers to accompany him, Hugh rode away from Stratton leaving Brendon to continue training the younger squires and the new mounts who had recently arrived. Miles would accompany him on this occasion.

London was heaving with people from all walks of life. So too the Inn where they were staying and Miles found he would be sharing a chamber with his lord and his body servant, much to his apprehension. Hugh warned Miles of thieves or slit purses, who targeted unsuspecting travellers and to make note of the landmarks so he would not get lost should they become separated. For the young squire, the whole experience was somewhat overwhelming but he soaked up the atmosphere like a sponge.

As the de Audley party made ready for the forthcoming Parliament, in the royal apartments Marguerite, Queen of England, sat back on the heavily cushioned chair and closed her eyes, pregnancy was not a condition she enjoyed overmuch. She waved her hands in a dismissive gesture and as her ladies began to leave the chamber, she spoke softly to Lady Ankaret.

'Stay, I wish to speak to you on a private matter.'

Dutifully the young woman remained as she was bade. Marguerite opened her vivid blue eyes and focused on the figure before her.

'It has come to my attention, Lady Ankaret, that you are conducting an illicit relationship with a married member of my husband's court.' She waited to see the impact her words had on her waiting woman. Ankaret blushed and dropped her head so the Queen could not see her expression. She did not answer the charge.

'As your Queen, I cannot condone such behaviour. It is a mortal sin and you stand in danger of losing your immortal soul. For the sake of the church and my husband, it is my duty to ensure that I maintain standards expected and therefore must take steps to safeguard your position here at court.' She paused allowing her words to find their mark. Still Ankaret remained silent.

'You have no words of defence?'

Finally, Ankaret raised her head. Her eyes were full of tears.

'I do not feel I have sinned for I love ......'

The Queen raised her hand to silence the speaker.

'The sin of adultery is a mortal sin as laid down in the laws of God and His holy church, what *you* feel counts for naught.' Her words were icy in their intensity. 'If you continue with this *liaison* I shall have no option but to send you home and you know that will be looked on with suspicion. Your very reputation and that of your family may come into question because of your selfishness. Do you understand?'

'Yes, your highness.' She stammered.

'Go and contemplate your future, if not for yourself then for your paramour, for he will be made to suffer also. Maybe not in the same way but nevertheless, his name will be besmirched.'

Ankaret Dampierre made an untidy curtsey and hurried from the chamber. Marguerite let out a deep sigh, her back ached and she felt tired but she judged that she had dealt with a delicate matter in the best way possible – directly and without rancour.

As the distraught Frenchwoman hastened away from the Queen's chamber, she encountered the handsome figure of Piers Gaveston. He grinned wickedly.

'Your sins have finally found you out.'

'So, it was you who told the Queen. I hate you!' She ran as fast as she could away from the grinning youth. Ankaret felt her heart was breaking and all she wanted to do was tell her lover about her interview with the Queen but when she did tell him later that day his reaction was not the one she had expected or hoped for, in fact, quite the opposite.

'Of course, I do not want you to leave England but we cannot defy the wishes of the Queen.'

Ankaret stared at Hugh in disbelief. 'I would, and have, defied everything to be with you. How can you so meekly submit? I thought you would have fought a little harder to keep me.'

Hugh realised he had made a serious mistake and desperately tried to extricate himself.

'Well – of course I meant for the time being, until we are no longer under suspicion. You know how much I love you.'

She looked at him, a contemptuous expression etched across her pretty features.

'No, no your response was not one of a man in love but of one discovered in his sin.'

She rose and was about to leave when he caught her in his arms but she beat her fists against his breast. 'Do not try to stop me I want no more of you.' With that, she broke away and ran weeping from the scene leaving Hugh bewildered by what had just transpired.

Later, when Ankaret returned to the Queen's chamber, Marguerite could see the girl had been crying but she carried out her duties silently. A distasteful incident, but one, which Marguerite felt had been necessary.

The rest of Hugh's stay in London was equally unsatisfactory with the bitter wrangling in Parliament continuing into April. However, Edward eventually gained ground and was now planning yet another excursion into Scotland later that summer. The news plunged Hugh into an even deeper mood of gloom. He had lost his lover and the pending plans for more warfare in the north meant more debt. He arrived at Stratton to discover yet another calamity, and one, which struck at his heart even more deeply than the loss of Lady Ankaret. His beloved daughter, Kate, had fallen ill and on the evening of his return home had died in his arms.

The whole household mourned the passing of the tiny girl whose bright, red-gold hair, bright eyes and winning personality, had made her such a loveable child. Isolde was inconsolable and sobbed so hard Ela was afraid she would follow her child to the grave. It was not uncommon to lose a child but Kate had been such a special little girl, beloved by both parents and in their loss, they found a bond of grief that drew them together.

The evening before the funeral, the couple sat together before the fire. Hugh took Isolde's hands and said softly, 'I have a confession to make and it is one that is so hard to speak of.'

Isolde could see he was struggling and when he continued his voice was thick with emotion. 'I know you will never forgive me but I fear, Kate died for my sins.'

Isolde remained silent for she could see the abject misery etched across his face.

'I took a mistress and therefore sinned against you and God and I believe this is His punishment, to take our little daughter from us.'

There was a long silence before Isolde spoke. 'Why should I be punished for your sin for my heart is broken too? Besides, I knew of your infidelity long ago.' She loosed his hold on her hand and rose and walked closer to the fire, twisting the rings on her fingers as she did so. 'If you think that Kate's death is your punishment then why have I been doubly punished?'

Hugh sat with his head bowed. 'That I cannot answer but feel that I am the sole cause of this loss. Why did you not challenge me on the matter before?'

'Because, what good would it have done? The affair had already begun and knowing you, being faced with the truth would have only driven you further away.' She paused. 'Do you feel that God is so vengeful?' Again, another long pause, 'it is a sad fact that children die just as easily as adults do. Why, look at your own aunt, the Countess of Lincoln, she has lost two sons to tragic accidents. Are you saying that she was a sinner?'

'No, of course not!' Hugh said harshly. He stood and moved closer to her neither speaking or moving for what seemed like an age. They just stood, neither wishing to break the silence. His flash of defiance melted as he said softly.

'Will you ever forgive me?'

'How do you think it made me feel to know you had taken another woman to your bed? I am a Mortimer, even though I am a bastard - do you think I have no pride?' Her voice was full of passion. She began to pace still twisting her fingers. 'My instinct was to seek vengeance but I sought guidance and so, I remained silent.' She turned to look at him. 'Maybe one day I will find it within me to forgive you but I will never forget or trust you again.' She came and stood before him and looked up into his eyes.

'I have been told love comes unbidden but accept our marriage was one of convenience however, I had always hoped, if not lovers, we could enjoy an amicable relationship. If you wish to put your immortal soul into danger for the sake of the French woman, I will pose no vocal objections,' Isolde wiped a tear from her dark eyes. She paused then added in little more than a whisper.

'But we do make lovely children together and I mourn the loss of our only daughter and will do so until the day I die. I know we share this grief and somehow with time, maybe we can forge a new relationship – this time built on honesty.' She left him standing in the light of the flickering flames too full of emotion to continue.

Ela could see Isolde had been weeping and she came and put her arms around the grief stricken figure.

'Oh, Ela, he has admitted his affair and believes it is the cause of Kate's death. He thought by admitting his transgression, I will absolve him but I ..... I cannot and told him exactly how I felt.' Isolde looked like a small child after being punished. Ela hugged her more closely.

'There, there, at least you both know what is in each other's hearts now. Come, have a sip of wine and get ready for bed, I will stay with you tonight.'

After a fitful night, Isolde emerged the following morning in black, ready for the funeral of her daughter. Dark smudges under her eyes denoted her lack of sleep and she took the arm of her husband flanked by their two sons. She looked neither right nor left and kept her eyes fixed on the tiny coffin. There were sounds of sobbing in the church. Isolde shivered, the church was cold and she felt an icy chill creep into her heart as she listened to the service of the dead, the Requiem Mass. Everyone who attended that service witnessed the grief of the family and admired the self-control of all four of its members.

Within days, Isolde began to arrange a visit to Pembridge and the Dowager Lady Mortimer. Maudie had written to say she had been ill recently and planned a visit, suggesting Isolde join her. It was a perfect opportunity to leave Stratton for a while at least. The raw emotion she felt made for an uneasy situation between her and her husband especially after James and Hugh had returned to court.

On a warm May morning, Isolde and her party rode out of the gates of Stratton with barely a backward glance. The further they went the better she felt and began to look forward to meeting Maudie again. She knew life must continue and tried to focus on the flowers, birds and springtime smells that pervaded the air. When they arrived at Pembridge Maudie was already there and came to greet them.

'Grandee is much better today. I'm sure she is looking forward to seeing you both again.'

Maudie hugged Isolde and Ela. 'We have had Mass said for Katherine and candles have been lit.'

'It is good to see you again,' murmured Isolde.

'With Grandee being so frail these days, the household is quite small but as you can imagine, runs very efficiently.' She grinned. 'What else would you expect?'

'I hope our visit will not over tire her.'

'Of course not, dearest Ela, she has been talking about you both since I suggested the visit.'

When they entered the hallway, they could see flowers arranged on dark wooden tables and the glow of rush lights lit up the darkest corners. The chamber of Maud de Braose, Dowager Lady Mortimer, was warm and comfortable, fresh rushes on the floor gave off a woody perfume and the gillie flowers in bowls, a sweet fragrance.

'Welcome to Pembridge, I am unable to walk far these days so forgive my tardiness in not greeting you at the door.' She peered hard at Isolde. 'My, you look so thin. We will have to take extra care of you whilst you are here. It is sad to lose anyone but especially a child, heaven knows, I suffered greatly when Ralph died.' She held out her hands in greeting and Isolde knelt as she kissed the long, white wrinkled fingers.

'Ela, it has been so long since last I saw you, we must make this visit special for all of us.'

Ela curtseyed but Lady Mortimer held out her hands so she too could kiss them.

So began a visit that would remain in the memories of all the women. For Isolde, she had a chance to speak of her life and to tell Maud, she understood how difficult it must have been to raise another woman's child. She confessed the mixed feelings her husband's affair had caused her. Towards the end of their stay, Isolde begged for forgiveness for her childhood behaviour, only to hear - there was nothing to forgive.

'My dear child, you have proved you are worthy to be called Mortimer's daughter. Albeit, at the time, you were a misfit but now, I can see much of your father in you and he, for all his faults, was a courageous warrior and knight. Never forget Isolde, he chose to acknowledge you as his own and that is all that matters now.'

For Ela, the visit was to make her farewell's to a woman she had loved and respected for many years. The two women talked privately and Maud thanked Ela for her loyalty to Isolde.

'I do not think we shall meet again this side of the grave and I am indebted to you for your service to Isolde. She is a complex character but is turning into a worthwhile one and for that, I thank God.'

As for young Maudie, she could see how frail her Grand-dam was and took care to tell her how much she loved and had always loved her.

'Ever my rock, and the valiant heart of our family. I know you do not fear death and if you do not wish to be buried at Wigmore, I will endeavour to have you buried either here or at Radnor, where I know you were happy. No doubt there will be a battle but for you my dearest Grandee, but I would face Satan himself to fulfil your wishes.'

'Hush now child, it matters not where they place my bones, my spirit will find its home.'

She smiled wryly. 'Some will say I do not deserve to enter the gates of heaven but, I have a feeling that Saint Peter is not brave enough to deny me entrance.'

Maudie had embraced her namesake and the two had stayed locked in each other's embrace for many minutes, both had tears in their eyes.

'You have always had my heart Maudie. I see much of me in you and am only sad that you have never found true love for, I can say in all honesty, that is the greatest prize life can offer. Now, let us part in smiles and not tears. My prayers go with you and am glad that you and Isolde remain close.'

It was the last time they would see Lady Mortimer but were not surprised that before she died, she had set in motion the wheels for a prestigious marriage for her grandson, Edmund's eldest son, Roger, to Joan de Geneville, heiress to Ludlow Castle.

Upon her return to Stratton, Isolde appeared subdued but plunged herself into the duties of her station and before Hugh left for Scotland the two had resumed a marital relationship. She knew of his fears regarding this new Scottish excursion. The deep division between the king and his subjects with regard to the Forest Charter, was the sticking point. Both sides were entrenched and without the king agreeing to recognize the boundaries that were in place before Henry III had encroached on them for his hunting grounds, nothing would change. The men needed for his Scottish campaign would not be available, neither would the taxes which were essential to fund the war. All she could do was to pray for the wars to be over and that life should find a more peaceful plain. Besides, her eldest son would soon be of an age to go to war and this knowledge filled her with fear, she could not lose another child.

However, her fears increased when she received a letter from Hugh which stated, although they had successfully taken Caerlaverock Castle, the number of desertions since had so depleted the English forces, they had fallen back. Naturally, he did not state exactly where they were in case the letter had fallen into enemy hands but the news disturbed her. It would leave the king's army vulnerable and she offered up a prayer for their safe deliverance.

As Isolde mulled over her letter, Hugh and his squires found themselves camped at a place called Sweetheart Abbey.

'It is ironic that we are in such a pleasant sounding place when our position is far from pleasing.' The irony of the situation was about to be compounded by the unexpected arrival of Robert Winchelsea, Archbishop of Canterbury, His mission was so important that he had taken the hazardous journey to deliver the Pope's letter himself. Edward Plantagenet read the long letter from the Holy See, which left him in an unenviable position, for the Pope had ordered him to 'leave' Scotland alone and to desist from further bloodshed admonishing him for the former acts of war against an independent nation. In a mood of subdued fury, Edward, faced with this latest setback, set sail for England, leaving the rest of his knights and nobles to make their own way back across the Border.

Hugh and his squires broke camp, and along with a number of other nobles, rode south just as the weather was beginning to show signs of autumn and the long days, now shortened into longer hours of darkness and biting frosts.

One evening around the campfire, Brendon broke the silence.

'I know Caerlaverock was a victory and there were acts of valour and courage on both sides but I cannot shake the feeling of disappointment for I felt it flew in the face of knightly chivalry.' No one spoke. 'There was no honour for those sixty men who had held the English army at bay for some considerable time. Surely, they should have been acknowledged for their bravery and not hung like common criminals.'

Hugh cleared his throat. 'Not all were hung Brendon, and remember what the Scots did to Cressingham and a number of English sheriffs. Edward Plantagenet is not a man to forget and he had to make an example.'

One of the older men spoke up. 'Chivalry died on the field of Evesham.' He paused to let his words take effect. 'You young ones forget, the king is also a Crusader and witnessed acts of unspeakable brutality on both sides during his years abroad. I know, I served under Lord L'Strange. We all learned the bitter lesson of our Infidel enemies. You do not allow your enemies to live, less they rise up to kill you at a later time.'

It opened the door to much debating of the rights and wrongs of the Scottish venture. Until they exhausted the subject, at least, for the time being and Brendon could see that his notion of the laws of chivalry may now, only be seen on the fields of the tournament and not on the fields of battle.

'At least we made a pretty spectacle with the banners and pennants flying in the breeze at Caerlaverock. You will have to put your more genteel feelings aside, young Brendon, if you are to serve Edward of England.'

'I think you are right Tom but now that the Pope has ordered the cessation to the wars in Scotland, do you think it will affect the king's future plans in the north?'

Tom chuckled. 'This king will not be deflected from his purpose, not even by the Pope, methinks, but time will tell. Now let us seek our beds.'

Brendon smiled wryly. 'At least we should be home before the winter sets in.' Brendon tried to keep his voice cheerful but he felt disillusioned by the events of the past weeks and his feelings did not change on the homeward journey.

BOOK TWO

DESTINY'S WHEEL

CHAPTER XVIII

Windsor
Winter of 1300/1

James de Audley looked down at the prone figure of his brother. 'Pray, what are you doing?' The younger boy did not reply but remained, his head bowed to hide his tears. A voice rang out from the other side of the courtyard.

'He was tripped by that weasel, De Spenser.' Piers Gaveston walked over and extended his hand for the boy to grasp. 'Young Hugh was carrying a tray of drinks when it happened, and as he fell, the whole lot splashed over the Prince, staining his garments. Had I not witnessed the incident from that window your brother would have been punished.' He grinned. 'I sent the little worm off with a flea in his ear but think you will have to watch out for your brother in future.'

'We are in your debt, my Lord Gaveston.' James studied the handsome figure of the Gascon.

'No debt, the de Audley family have my respect and I will not see any one of them brought low by a cowardly act.'

James bowed. 'Nevertheless I ..... we, appreciate your timely assistance.'

Piers nodded as he looked at Hugh. 'Well, you had better replenish the wine for when the Prince returns.' Hugh scrambled to his feet and rushed away to do as he was bid. Gaveston turned to speak to James.

'I have noticed you at sword practice and commend your progress. Maybe you would join me one morning. Your late uncle took me under his wing when first I came to England and feel it only fitting I return his act of kindness.'

James smiled shyly. 'I am afraid you will find me be but a poor adversary, I will have to practice many months before I come anywhere near your skills, my Lord Gaveston.'

'Nonsense, you are far better than you give yourself credit for! Besides, I tire of my current partner, he is so predictable, and I find him no challenge at all these days.'

'Then I shall be at your service on the morrow. And thank you again for your intervention with my brother.'

Piers Gaveston watched the older de Audley youth walk back into the castle. Could this be another possible candidate to recruit to the Prince's royal circle? Mortimer had already proved a worthy member, albeit he was younger than either the Prince or Gaveston but had all the attributes which would be required for the future, when the Prince became King. It may prove to be a good move to add the de Audley brothers although. Hugh was far too young at this moment in time. However, it would do no harm to cultivate the boy, with the future in mind. If the Prince, recently created '*Prince of Wales*', appeared to give his role as heir little thought, his close companion never stopped planning. The recent campaign in Scotland had been an enlightening experience for Gaveston. He had come to realise that without his urging the Prince, although ostensibly in command of a battalion, had proved he had but scant perception of what the role entailed. He had been the one to *suggest,* urge and steer the young prince through the campaign. Gaveston was quite aware of his growing power and he intended to use it for the good of young Edward but also, to enhance his own standing at court.

Lady Ankaret Dampierre had also witnessed the scene in the courtyard, and as she moved back from the casement window she murmured, 'I see my Lord Gaveston is up to mischief again.'

Queen Marguerite sighed. She was pregnant with her second child and her normal even temper had deserted her. 'Lady Ankaret, I must remind you that Lord Gaveston was appointed as companion to Prince Edward by the king and therefore, holds a position of some note. I will not have you constantly pointing the finger of suspicion in his direction, do you understand?'

The rebuke rankled and Ankaret turned her face so her expression of fury was not witnessed by anyone else in the chamber. She bobbed a curtsey and nodded.

'As you command, Highness.' She busied herself with folding silk ribbons and kept her eyes averted. Inwardly she vowed to continue with her campaign to undermine Gaveston's reputation since she had discovered, he had been the one who had told the Queen of her affair with Lord de Audley.

Completely unaware of the scene between the Queen and her lady in waiting Gaveston had walked to the stables to seek the Prince who was busily shoeing his favourite horse.

'Ah, there you are Piers.' The tall handsome figure let go of the horse's hoof he had been working on and grinned, beads of sweat glistened on his brow.

'You know, it is so satisfying knowing I am as competent now as Gilbert.'

'Then Gilbert better watch out or you may take his place.'

The two friends laughed together as Gilbert looked on sheepishly. He could never quite believe that the future heir to the throne spent so much of his time in the stables or, with the builders and masons employed maintaining the royal residences. He took the lead rope and led the great horse away to his stable as the two youths strolled back towards the castle, deep in conversation. As he walked back into the darkness of the stable, he patted the gleaming neck of the stallion and whispered.

'A strange brotherhood is it not? Still that is not for us to worry our heads about my beauty, we just serve the noble house of Plantagenet.' He gathered an armful of sweet smelling hay, and threw it into the manger, then continued with his duties.

As Gilbert resumed his stable work Gaveston and the Prince were making plans to travel to Langley, a favoured residence of the young Plantagenet heir.

'I need to school the young horse I purchased before we left; I believe he has the makings of a fine charger.'

'Really Piers, you spend so much time schooling your horses and practising with your sword and lance I scarce see you during the daytime.'

Gaveston made a face. 'Maybe if you spent more time in like pursuits and less with the masons and builders and such you would not make so many mistakes. Remember, your enemies will not give you chance to re-mount in the field of battle, nor will they allow you to pick up your weapons. Besides, dear friend, I do it so that I will be able to defend you, so instead of complaining you should show me more gratitude.'

The expression on Edward's face spoke more eloquently than words and Gaveston relented and clapped his companion of the shoulder. 'Fear not, you continue with your plebeian pursuits and leave the knightly duties to me if it gives you pleasure. However, I do think it would prove beneficial if we took along a few of the younger squires to hone their knightly skills out of the sight of the older knights who make fun of their younger contemporaries.'

Edward smiled. 'Does that mean you will have all the pleasure of making fun of them to yourself?'

Gaveston's face grew serious. 'No, that is not my aim.' But he would not be drawn on the topic at this moment with the Prince, for he wanted to see if he had chosen wisely for the extra training.'

'Who do you have in mind to accompany us?'

'Well, young Mortimer and the eldest de Audley were two that spring to mind and maybe, young Damory.'

'Excellent! I look forward to seeing their progress under your tuition.'

The days at Langley were busy and Gaveston was true to his word, he kept the young squires hard at practice from morning until mid afternoons alternating between practising with the lance on horseback and on foot with the sword.

One afternoon, as the exhausted trio lay back on the grass, after finishing a hard bout of hand to hand fighting Roger Mortimer sat up and rubbed his forearm.

'I swear my arm has grown since I arrived.' He sat flexing his arm as he spoke. 'Do you think with all this hard practising, we will ever gain praise for our efforts?' He looked across at his companions.

'It is not my arms that ache, but my arse!' Damory exclaimed ruefully.

'And I feel as though my shoulders and thighs will burst into flames at any moment.'

None had heard Gaveston move towards them.

'Knights do not whinge at a little pain.'

The trio, sat bolt upright as his approached and groaned in unison.

'Have mercy my Lord Gaveston, battles do not last for more than a day, unless it is a siege.'

'Gentlemen, you may complain now but one day, you will be grateful for my insistence, pain is part of the learning process and how to manage it. It is your mind as well as your brawn that I endeavour to expand; to overcome discomfort, whether at a tourney or a battlefield. It is an essential part of your training. However, tomorrow we shall go hunting as I am pleased with the progress you have all made.' He gave a wicked grin then walked back to join the waiting Prince.

'Well Piers, give me your verdict.' Edward said as he fell in step with his friend.

'All three have come on better than I expected but two are quite exceptional, young Mortimer and Damory; de Audley is not far behind, in fact, mounted he is better than the two Rogers'.'

'So you are pleased with your young protégés?'

'More than pleased but will not tell them that. I have promised them a day's hunting tomorrow.'

'Good! Now let me show you what I have been doing whilst you have been busy with your trainees.'

The time at Langley had not only been to hone the skills of the young squires but also, to help then form a bond of friendship. Mortimer and de Audley, who were related by blood, Damory, was a brother in arms and the coming years would both strengthen and test that bond.

Upon their return, as they entered the courtyard, a figure darted forward and caught the bridle of James de Audley.

'I have been watching for you to come.' The freckled face of the younger de Audley looked troubled.

'What ails you?' James swung easily out of his saddle and handed the reins to the waiting groom. 'Has Despenser, been bullying you again?'

'No, no, nothing like that.' Hugh looked anxiously about him before speaking again. 'But he and the Lady Dampierre have been whispering in corners whilst you were away and I overheard part of a conversation.' Hugh's freckled face was full of concern. Before he could continue, the Prince and Gaveston had joined the group.

'Well, go on; do not leave us in suspense, pray.' Lord Gaveston moved closer to the boy.

'They are plotting against you my Lord, I could not hear any details only your name and *downfall ere long*.'

Gaveston threw back his head and laughed. 'Did you hear that Ned? The Weasel and the French Wench are planning my downfall.'

'I'll have him dismissed from court.' There was no disguising the anger in the Prince's voice.

'May I suggest another ploy? Why not and turn the tables on the unsuspecting pair.'

There was a murmur of agreement among the squires.

Hugh's boyish voice piped up. 'I can watch and report on them as I have been made page to the Queen.'

James put his hand on his brother's shoulder. 'You would have to be careful and not get caught.'

Indignantly, Hugh pulled himself up to his full height. 'I managed whilst you were absent did I not?'

Gaveston grinned mischievously. 'I believe you can do this Hugh and will learn much from the experience.'

The Prince appeared pleased with the plan. 'We will all keep our eyes and ears open, not only for the Despenser but, for anyone who would plot against Piers.'

As the party began to split up Roger Mortimer fell in step with the two de Audley brothers.

'If you have any trouble with Despenser let me know for it would give me great pleasure to bloody his nose.'

James frowned. 'I can take care of my brother.'

'Of that I have no doubt but you cannot always be there especially when you are on duty. We can easily arrange our rotas to ensure that one of us is free.'

'Count me in.' Damory chimed in as he joined them, 'it will be easier with three of us.'

Therefore, it was agreed, they would take turns in watching out for young Hugh.

'You may find it difficult Hugh to remain silent and listen, for I know how you love to chatter.'

'Discipline is one of the major rules in all walks of life but especially if you wish to be a good soldier and knight, so it will not hurt Hugh to learn this valuable lesson.' Roger Mortimer's voice was low and serious.

James smiled wryly. 'Oh, you have no idea what a hard lesson it will be for him but, he has managed to fulfil the role so far,' He clapped his brother on the back as he spoke.

Their plan would unite the young squires more closely in the coming days.

Later that month, Roger Mortimer learned of the death of his beloved grand-dam, Maude de Braose, the dowager Lady Mortimer. The roads were too bad to reach the Marches in time for her funeral. He went to chapel the following morning and lit a candle and prayed for the woman who had brought alive the exploits of his family; especially with regard to his grand-sire, Sir Roger Mortimer, the hero of the Battle of Evesham and of her grand-sire, the legendary knight, William Marshal. It had been Maud who had suggested a marriage between their neighbour's, granddaughter, Joan de Geneville and himself, which would, in the future, bring the Castles and lands in not only of Ludlow but also, Trim in Ireland and estates in France. Life would be the poorer for her passing and he felt a deep sense of personal loss.

As the young Mortimer prayed for his dead grand-dam, another member of the family struggled with her emotions, at the news, Isolde Mortimer. As a girl, she had caused a lot of disruption for the woman she felt was her enemy. However, in her adult years and in light of the events of her own life, she viewed Maud's role in her childhood in a new light. In retrospect, Maud had armed her with all the schooling necessary for her current role in life and had also, led by example. She had armed her ward with the weapons, which Isolde silently acknowledged, now stood her in good stead.

Isolde arranged for Masses to be said at Stratton, although would not face the uncertainty of the journey to Pembridge.

However, she did send a letter of condolence to Maudie, whom she knew would be deeply upset by the news. In private, Isolde and Ela prayed for the departed soul of Maud de Braose and each mourned her in their own way.

Soon after, a break in the weather saw Stratton returned to a normal rhythm of life. However, it saw the departure of Lord Hugh who had recently, been joined by his sons. James, had been given leave after the intense training at Langley. The Queen had also given young Hugh permission to accompany his brother.

In the months to come, their lives would be far from a normal. Hugh senior, was to return to the king's household together with his young son and namesake, who would be returning to his duties in the Queen's household, whilst James, would re-join the Prince's retinue.

From the letters Isolde received from her younger son, Hugh, he appeared to have gained a favoured position with the Queen and she felt a sense of pride that the three men in her life had all achieved places of trust in their respective households and she prayed for their health and safety during these uncertain times. The visit had been all too brief, just a few days where the de Audley family could spend time together and Isolde cherished those days with her sons.

CHAPTER XIX

End of Lent 1301

As the winter began to loosen its grip, and the first spring flowers opened, the younger squires of the king's court were given leave to go home for Eastertide. Among their numbers were the de Audley brothers, who were accompanied by Roger Mortimer, and Roger Damory. They made all speed towards the mid lands and chatted easily together as they rode, teasing young Hugh unmercifully. As the party neared Oxfordshire, James invited his companions to spend at least one night with his family. The offer was eagerly accepted and as they clattered into the courtyard of Stratton, the Lady Isolde hurried forward to greet them.

'Welcome, welcome. There is food in the Hall, although it is mainly fish as we are still fasting. I will have extra beds made up for you all.'

James leapt off his horse, and ran to his mother as he bent to kiss her on both cheeks, followed by young Hugh who flung his arms around his mother. Mortimer and Damory remained mounted and watched the scene of reunion with a mixture of amusement and embarrassment.

'Mama, may I introduce you to Roger Damory and our kinsman, Roger Mortimer.' James held his mother's arm as he guided her to the where the riders sat.

'I have seen you before on a visit to Wigmore some years ago, but you have grown out of all recognition.' She smiled up at the young Mortimer as she spoke. 'You are both most welcome to spend the night with us. I hardly dared hope I would be seeing you again so soon.'

The two Rogers' dismounted, and came and kissed the hand of their hostess.

'You are most generous Lady de Audley.' Mortimer had taken the lead.

'Come and refresh yourselves and we will eat as soon as you are ready.' Isolde smiled at her handsome young guests as she led the way into the castle.

During the course of the evening Isolde learned of the progress of her sons but when young Hugh started to tell her about the visit to Langley, James nudged him and flashed a warning glance in an effort to silence his chatter.

'I think Mama would be more interested in learning more about your duties with the Queen, Especially now that you have become one of her favourite pages, is that not so Mama?' James looked across at his mother whilst giving his young brother a kick under the table. 'It will be of far more interesting than hearing of our daily weaponry practise.'

Hugh blushed he realised he had spoken too freely and had almost revealed that James and his friends were part of the Prince's inner circle. A fact not to be shared with anyone, not even his mother. Later, Isolde played and sang for a while, then suggested her young guests amuse themselves with board games until bedtime.

'I feel there is a secret that these young squires share and one poor Hugh almost let slip but what it is.........' Isolde's spoke to herself but Ela heard and noted her concern.

'At their age, the mystery of growing into manhood may bind them but I am sure if you get Hugh on his own, he will not be able to hold such a secret from you.'

'We shall see Ela. We shall see.'

The following day Damory and Mortimer rode off towards their own homes to spend precious time with their respective families. Life at Stratton had a much more vibrant air with the return of its younger members. James spent hours with his sword and in the tiltyard, watched by his brother and father. He was able to demonstrate the improvements he had made and much to his surprise gained praised for his prowess.

On Easter morning, the family attended church but afterwards, they broke their fasting and enjoyed a feast. The merry making continued for many hours until exhausted, they all sought their beds with full bellies and happy hearts.

However, the time together was all too short and when James and Hugh, and their father, rode through the gates, Isolde waved her farewells but felt a sense of misgiving as she turned to walk back into the castle.

As events would show, Isolde's intuitions would prove to be well founded. Hugh senior and junior headed to Canterbury whilst his son, James rode to join the Prince who had recently been invested as Prince of Wales by his father. Edward headed to his Welsh lands and later to the Marches to recruit men for the forthcoming Scottish campaign. At his side, rode Piers Gaveston, Roger Mortimer, Roger Damory, and James de Audley.

Gaveston was in high good humour, the thought of action appealed to his adventurous nature. It was time to put into practice all the months of training, for the squires and their mettlesome stallions.

April, saw the young Prince and his followers riding to Kenilworth, where they were to join the king. All that is, but Roger Mortimer, who would be returning to Wigmore in readiness for his marriage later in the year.

The long months of wrangling over the Charters had been mostly resolved. Now, with the return of the Earl of Lincoln from his visit to Rome, the king's spirits rose. The letters from Pope Boniface VIII, gave the king, means to raise much needed taxes. The way was opening for the king to bring Scotland under his control. He discussed his strategy with his commanders and this time, the decision was to split the army into two; he would be in command of one army whilst his son the other. The plan was to use a pincer movement along the Border from one coastline to the other. Then they would re-unite their armies at Stirling, thus giving their enemies no means of escape.

The walls of Kenilworth Castle echoed with the sound of steel on steel and the neighing of horses, mingled with the shouts of the knights in the lists. The excitement, as they sharpened their skills in readiness for the forthcoming campaign in the north, was tangible. The King and Queen enjoyed days hunting even though pregnant, Marguerite still refused to give up her favourite pastime. There was a distinct hum about the castle and the king felt certain this time, the Plantagenet banners, would be carried to victory, at the head of his English forces.

Edward began to make plans for the forthcoming fight and although he had given his son the command of his own army, the king had ensured that his old friend and advisor, Henry de Lacy, Earl of Lincoln, would accompany the Prince. De Lacy was a seasoned soldier who held the respect of his men, a vital ingredient for the difficult days ahead.

By June, the armies had reached the Borders and the king ordered his officers to admit the 'middle men' of Scotland to the king's peace. It was a strategic move to bring not only more men to the king's standard but also, much needed funds.

The Prince with his troops reached Carlisle on the 24th June where he began to muster more men to his army whilst his father, headed to Berwick reaching his destination by early July. A contingent from Ireland landed at Arran on the 15th July swelling the rank by some 2000 men. By the 18th of July Sir Adam Welle, keeper of the castle, sent six crossbowmen for twelve days service. In late July, the Scots captured one of the crossbowmen, on the very day of the king arrival in Peebles.

Ayr Castle fell to the Prince and the Earl of Lincoln, who garrisoned it, leaving Sir Montasini de Novelliano, as its Constable. Turnberry also fell to the English, both de Brus strongholds. The latter, being Robert's birthplace. The English also took the Comyn Castle of Dalswinton, which lay close to Dumfries.

Meanwhile, the king's army seized Bothwell, which was subsequently granted to Sir Aymer de Valence, the Earl of Pembroke. In late August, a mutiny broke out at Berwick due to lack of wages and men began to desert in large numbers, echoes of the previous campaign in Scotland. The king raged against his chancellors to whom he sent urgent messages for funds.

As for Sir Hugh de Audley, he was given the command of Keeper of Selkirk Forest, a hideout for the Scottish rebels. A command which kept him and his men busy, keeping the Scots contained whilst preventing others on entering into the sanctuary of the thick undergrowth. However, the plans to unite the English armies, was thwarted by a Scottish force, which harried the king's army, thus forcing him to abandon his former tactics. The Scots strategy, was most likely ordered by, one of the Guardians, Sir John Soules, who had taken over from Sir John Comyn and Sir Ingram d'Umfraville earlier that year.

Edward Plantagenet was beginning to find his position almost untenable, with daily desertions and lack of vivers. It was a relief, when in mid September whilst at Berwick, Sir John Droxford, Keeper of the Wardrobe at the York exchequer, finally sent 2000 marks. One quarter was immediately sent to the Prince's men in Carlisle.

Meanwhile, the Prince had taken time out to go on a pilgrimage to St. Ninian's at Whithorn, but the Scots had removed the relics to the recently built, Sweeheart Abbey. Upon discovering the loss, the English had them returned to their original place. Whilst the Prince and Gaveston worshipped in the ancient church, two of the band of three squires, had time to relax.

'It looks as though we will be spending the winter here in Scotland.' Damory's tone was flat and the murmurs of agreement from his companion left them feeling deflated. As James unfastened his scabbard, he drew his sword to check the blade.

'I knew I had blunted the blade on that Scotsman's thick skull.'

'Well at least he won't be troubling us anymore.' Damory grinned.

'I wonder how my father is getting on at Selkirk,' James had picked up his bacinet to inspect as he spoke, but the fears of the young squires, were to prove unfounded. Henry de Lacy sent word, that the services of many of the younger knights would not be required throughout the winter. Gaveston was unhappy with this new turn of events but could do nothing more than complain to the Prince, for even he knew that Ned was little more than a figurehead and that de Lacy was the real 'puppet master'.

'Well I for one am pleased to be going home, the thought of spending a cold, frugal winter here in Scotland, kicking our heels, held naught but misery for me.' It was Damory, who voiced the thoughts of his compnaion.

'At least Mortimer must be having a much better time for he will have much celebrating to do at his wedding. The Lady Joan de Geneville is quite a catch, I hear. Whereas here I fear, many will be eating their own horses if the food supplies do not get through.'

'Well I for one would never eat my horse, he has served me well, and I would not treat a faithful servant thus.' James was vehement in his condemnation of such barbaric acts.

'He would probably be too tough anyway.' Quipped Damory, as he playfully punched James on the shoulder.

As the remainder of the Prince's army made ready to join the king and queen at Dunipace, a number of troops, plus wagons filled with wounded, accompanied by some of the younger squires, began the long and hazardous journey home.

'Well I wonder whether all that effort has been worth it!' Exclaimed Damory as they headed south.

'Many of the garrisons are too strung out to be defensible for long; lack of provisions due to their inland locations will make it hard for those who defend them.' The sobering words left them lost to their own thoughts.

'Besides, did I hear correctly, is the king trying to garner another truce?' It was Damory, who had eventually broken the silence. There was no answer only time would tell.

As they continued their long journey, word came that there had been a fierce fight at Airth, near Stirling, where a number of English horses, were killed. At the end of October a messenger bound for London, informed them that one of the soldiers from Berwick garrison, had been taken captive at Melrose, even though Sir Hugh de Audley had been sent extra troops, it appeared it had failed to stop an attack.

Eventually, the weary group headed for their homes, the wounded had been left at various monasteries along the route for further care. The two squires took their leave of each other promising to meet again upon the return of the king to court. It was a very tired party of travellers, who finally arrived at Stratton, to the relief of Isolde and Ela.

In the days that followed, Isolde learned of the hardships her son and his friends had suffered, over the summer as they fought to take strategic castles along the Borders. The question that burned on her lips was of the welfare of his father but apart from hearing that he had again requested more men, James had heard nothing more. Later, they learned that the Queen had travelled north.

'Now that the Queen has joined her husband do you think the hostilities will cease.'

James shook his head. 'My dearest Mama, hostilities never really cease. We take a castle, garrison it then move on. The Scots then re-take it and so it goes on.'

'No doubt young Hugh is with the Queen so maybe he will be able to spend Christmastide with his father.'

'Being Keeper of Selkirk Forest is not a titular title Mama, it is an important post, the place is where many of the Scots hide and re-group and therefore Father has to ensure this does not happen. I can assure you, it is no easy posting.'

'Then we must pray that he remains safe.' She paused. 'It does demonstrate the king's confidence in your father, so that must stand as a royal endorsement of his abilities.'

'I suppose you are right.' James smiled. 'The king ensured the Prince was supported by one of his most trusted advisors and friend, the Earl of Lincoln. In fact, it is Lincoln who really commands the Prince's army, Edward is but the figurehead.'

'The king merely looks to his son's safety. Besides, the lessons he is learning from a seasoned soldier will be invaluable when he becomes king.' Isolde had noted how James was beginning to act more like a man than a boy, and she felt a pang of nostalgia as she realised he would soon be old enough to take a wife, just as her young kinsman had done. It would mean a move to his own household and the thought left Isolde feeling a pang of sorrow.

James wanted to know if she had attended the wedding of the young Roger Mortimer at Pembridge.

'Indeed, it was a lavish affair and the couple looked nervous but happy.' Isolde smiled at the memory.

'I cannot believe that Mortimer is married. It will put a stop to his carefree lifestyle with his marital responsibilities.' James voice was thoughtful.

'It will be your turn soon.' Isolde smiled up at her son.

James frowned. 'I cannot say I look forward to marrying anyone for a while yet. I do not feel ready to share my life.'

'It is the natural order of things but as you say, your father and I have yet to find a suitable match.'

Isolde fell silent, the years passed so swiftly, it seemed no time since he was in swaddling clothes and here they were speaking of marriage. Shrugging off her feelings, Isolde changed the subject as she could see her son was uncomfortable with thoughts of the future. She suggested that they invite Lady Katherine, and her son Thomas, with Eve Clavering, the girl he was to marry, to spend the Festive Season with them at Stratton but Isolde would live to regret her charitable act in the months and years to come.

Upon the arrival of Lady Katherine Giffard and her son, Isolde was struck by the dramatic change in her sister-in-law. Katherine wore a stark, black kirtle and veil, over a white wimple and a thick black belt with a set of jet rosary beads hanging from it. The once handsome face was pale and gaunt, and it was obvious, she had lost a considerable amount of weight. Thomas also, looked wan and sickly and he wheezed like a broken winded nag. Only Eve appeared hale and hearty and in the full bloom of her girlhood.

After their initial greetings, the two women made their way into a side chamber where refreshments were set out on polished trestle tables.

'I was not expecting to see Eve.' Isolde looked across at the girl who was sipping a drink.

'It has all been somewhat of a trial. When Thomas was made ward of Hugh Despenser two years ago, I expected him to arrange a match with one of his daughters but .....' Katherine paused. 'Thomas was told in no uncertain terms by his son, that the Despenser family did not wish to be allied to a penniless invalid.'

Isolde's expression spoke volumes. 'I have heard that the young Despenser has the tongue of a viper and only Gaveston keeps him in check.'

'Thankfully, it has all worked out for the best as dear Eve, had refused to leave me after Thomas's departure. Once they are married I shall retire to an order of nuns at Ledbury and serve out my days in prayer and fasting.'

Isolde touched her hand. 'If that is your wish then, so be it.'

'I feel out of touch with this world since my husband's death and believe I can serve God and achieve salvation in his service.'

'Well, let us make the most of this visit and enjoy each other's company whilst we may.'

They chatted together discussing the birth of the Queen's second son, Edmund at Woodstock, earlier that year, which was only a day's ride from Stratton; and the state of the country. They also debated the effects of the new taxes were having but Isolde sensed that Katherine's mind was far away and that secular matters held but little interest to her now.

Isolde was heartened to see as the days passed, the colour begin to appear on the cheeks of Thomas and his energy increase. However, it was James and Eve, who were revelling in their time together and their laughter and joy echoed around the walls of Stratton. During the evenings, they danced and played board games, which Thomas could also join in and Isolde felt it was truly a season of wellbeing for the younger generation.

'The wars in Scotland seem so far away.' Isolde mused one evening.

Katherine Giffard nodded. 'I heard from Brendon in October. His wounds have healed but he will not be returning to England.'

Isolde frowned. 'I did not know he had left Scotland or that he was wounded.'

Katherine remained silent for a moment before continuing. 'He returned with the Irish contingent. Apparently, he left your husband's service after speaking his mind on a personal matter.'

'Oh! Did he expand on the reason?'

Katherine looked up and nodded. 'He said he felt he could no longer serve your husband in the knowledge of the adulterous affair with Lady Dampierre.'

Isolde let out a long sigh. 'Brendon was ever protective towards me and I shall miss him.'

'Nicolas had asked him to look after you knowing of his brother's uncertain temperament.'

The two women sat in silence for a while.

'His adultery puts his soul in mortal danger but his betrayal no longer hurts me it merely destroys any respect I had for him. I know you will not wish to hear such sentiments and advocate forgiveness but ....' Isolde's words trailed off.

'I understand more than you think, and do not either condemn, nor do I condone but will pray for you both.'

The Christmastide passed all too quickly and on the evening before their departure, James found himself alone with Eve.

'You will never know how much I have enjoyed being in your company.'

'Yes, it has been most pleasurable.' Eve's smile held a hint of sadness.

'Poor Thomas has so few days when he can ride out and it was a clever idea of Lady Isolde's, to hunt with the hawks last week, the day in the open air did help him with his breathing.'

'How do you feel about marrying someone who is more of an invalid than.......'

'When Thomas was made ward of Sir Hugh Despenser, my father ordered me home but Lady Katherine was in such low spirits I defied him and remained, because I felt I could be of help to her. She had been so kind to me and you see it worked out all right in the end. I would rather marry kindly Thomas, who I grew up with, than a stranger.'

'But what if you fell in love?'

'Pray, who would fall in love with me?'

James took her hand. 'Maybe I would.'

Eve snatched her hand away. 'You must not speak of such things James. However special you are to me but - love?'

'I know you are not yet old enough to marry and therefore may not understand such feelings but I know how I feel about you dearest Eva.'

Her face became serious. 'My name is Eve as you well know and although I have allowed you all to use my family's pet name for me, think it may be time to use my birth name in future, it may give me more gravitas. My feelings towards you can be nothing more than that of a dear friend. That is how it must and shall be - if you cannot accept this I must remove myself from your company.'

Alarmed, James rose, then dropped to one knee before her. 'I wanted you to know how I truly felt just in case I never see you again.'

Eve reached and touched his cheek. 'Please do not frighten me, I would miss you more than.....' He caught her hand and kissed it.

'My sweet little Eva.'

'Say no more but know you will be in my prayers.' There was a catch in her voice.

Eve rose and went to bed, her mind racing. The knowledge that James had such warm feelings towards her made her feel guilty and she lay awake far into the night struggling with her own emmotions.

The following day Lady Katherine and her party left Stratton. James went for a long ride trying to dispel his anxieties. Upon his return both Isolde and Ela noticed the change in him but neither realised the true reason and put it down to being alone once more. Within a week, James also left Stratton to resume his knightly duties at Windsor.

CHAPTER XX

1302
Stratton

The arrival of Hugh de Audley in early April changed the quiet routine for Isolde and Ela and it was soon clear his service in Scotland had not improved his temper. When pressed for details on his months away, he brushed aside the questions like flies on a summer's day. It was some time later, Isolde learned of the welfare of her young son and there was even a brief reference to Brendon's departure but no mention of cross words, merely that he had been wounded and had chosen to return to Ireland with the Irish mercenaries.

A few weeks later Isolde realised she was pregnant and suffered the mornings of sickness with a stoic resilience. It was difficult to gauge whether Hugh was pleased with the news of impending fatherhood for his mood was off hand and when not barking orders to his staff, he would spend long periods locked in his study dictating letters. However, he did take time to visit his sons at Windsor.

In late June, a messenger brought word that the Scots had broken the truce and had captured Edinburgh, putting all to the sword. However, the castle had resisted attack. The news galvanised Hugh into action and without little preamble he and a band of seasoned soldiers made ready to return once more to join the king in the north.

On the evening before his departure, Hugh did speak of events he had experienced whilst serving in Scotland and it became clear; it was mainly due to this, which lay at the root of his uncertain temper. In addition, the heavy drain the war was having on their finances was the cause of his many sleepless nights.

'I fear the lack of funds is having a far greater affect on events for all concerned. The king is constantly sending for money, which is either late in arriving or, not sufficient to pay all of his troops, hence the mass desertions. No one really blames them, for they would starve and resort to lawlessness, which sadly, is already happening on both sides.'

'Before your return home, I heard tell of hardships caused by the heavy handed methods of the requisitioning of supplies and livestock for the war. Do you think the king is aware of how this affects his people?' Isolde's tone was low and thoughtful.

'The king is playing a dangerous game with few, if any, aces in his hand. I do know, he will be making the best use of this period of the so called truce.'

'He must find it galling to have the French now involved.' Isolde looked at her husband's face to see his reaction.

'No doubt he will make his true feelings quite apparent to those who have remained with him.'

In July, after her husband's departure, word came from France that the Flemish army, had been victorious at the battle of Courtrai, which left Isolde wondering how this would affect the Scottish truce; France being Scotland's ally.

The days quickly turned into months and letters from her husband gave her brief glimpses of events happening in the north. In September, the man who had played a significant role as the king's lieutenant in the north, Sir John St. John, had died, his post had for the time being, been filled by his son and namesake. She also learned, that James had rejoined the Prince.

Isolde tried to keep abreast of her family's exploits in Scotland but found this pregnancy both irksome and uncomfortable as she suffered with searing back pains. Ela tried her best to find curatives and remedies to help but nothing seemed to work leaving Isolde to suffer sleepless nights, which caused a shortness of temper.

The Christmastide at Stratton that year was very quiet, Isolde had invited no one to share the festivities for she felt far from joyful and longed for the day she would be brought to bed, and delivered of this child. Ela bustled about trying to be as cheerful and positive in the hope it would raise the spirits of her Lady but her efforts prove fruitless.

In the last days of January, Isolde gave birth to a baby girl and felt an overwhelming wave of relief. Exhausted but triumphant she offered up a prayer of thanks and as she looked down at the tiny bundle, murmured to her how much suffering she had caused but she was a most welcomed member of the family. Church bells rang; Masses were said in rejoice of the birth. Ela offered up her personal thanks to the Almighty for giving Isolde another daughter. Once Isolde had received her forgiveness from the church in the age old tradition, she could once more resume her place back into society.

Soon afterwards, Maudie arrived in March, bearing gifts for the new baby and the two young women found great comfort in each other's company.

'Pray what name have you chosen? No doubt you discussed it with Hugh before he left.'

Isolde smiled. 'Yes we did, and chose Alice after the Countess of Lancaster, Alice de Lacy.'

Maudie nodded. 'She is certainly the finest Lady at the court and has none of the artifice the majority of women have who surround the royal family.'

'Maybe Alice will take her place at court one day.' Isolde said looking down at the sleeping child. They talked and speculated on the future of the new arrival, watched over by Ela.

'Do you expect Hugh to return any time soon?'

'I do not believe so, the last news I had was they were to muster at Berwick in May but think the shortage of supplies and money makes life very difficult for all, not only the king's army.'

Maudie remained at Stratton until the end of May by which time Isolde had regained her strength and energy and could be heard practising her music again. A sure sign, that the Lady of Stratton was once again feeling at one with the world.

Meanwhile in Scotland, Hugh had plunged back into the hectic world of border warfare. The strategy of chevauchees, which had proved so successful, was still in operation. Bands of armed men would ride out and attack the enemy when they least expected it, using the same hit and run tactics to great success; tactics used initially, by the Scots. Although the position of Keeper of Selkirk had been given to Sir Andrew Baliol. Hugh now found himself under the direct command of

Sir John Segrave, along with a number of other distinguished nobles, such as Robert Brus, the young Earl of Carrick. In early March, at a place called Happrew, near Peebles, the English were in a fierce skirmish against men, commanded by Sir Simon Fraser and Sir William Wallace. The latter had returned from France and had joined Fraser in the continuing struggle against their English foe. The king commended the action of his English troops.

Later that month, Edward called a Parliament at St. Andrew's, the first to be held in Scotland, since 1296. During this session, a number of Scottish landowners, together with the Bishop of Glasgow, swore fealty to the English king so, little by little Edward Plantagenet was gaining more support, albeit reluctantly in many instances.

Inevitably the stage was being set for a siege of Stirling Castle and Sir Alexander Livingstone the sheriff, was notified to prepare for the forthcoming attack. In April, siege engines were sent for and the great '*War Wolf*' was brought on site in readiness to rain death and devastation on the defiant occupants of the castle.

'You know Will, I swear I would not wish to awake each morning to face such a vicious foe as '*War Wolf*'.' Hugh said as he turned to Sir William Latimer. The two seasoned knights surveyed the scene before them as they steadied their restless mounts.

'Have you seen how the Greek Fire sends them running in confusion on the ramparts?' Sir William Latimer spoke in hushed tones. He continued, 'That is evil stuff, I saw someone who had been burned by it and the scars were both painful and ugly and did not heal as other burns.'

The two English noblemen watched for a while, then urged their horses forward to take up their positions for the day. The bombardments continued for two months until on the morning of the 24th July, Sir William Oliphant, surrendered the castle and along with his men were taken into captivity and sent back across the border in chains. The business began of repairing the castle for the victors. It had been a significant victory for the English which caused a great deal of chagrin amongst their Scottish adversaries.

To celebrate, the king announced there would be a tournament for all the knights and nobles to show off their prowess and enjoy their success. Hugh de Audley viewed the scene after his successful bout and felt a sense of pride as his he watched his son entered the arena. The trumpets blared and the crowd shouted their encouragement as the two knights chose their lances. The wind whipped the pennants and tents, which flapped and strained at the guy ropes.

'Your son is a fine horseman, for his charger is a handful.' Sir William Latimer's voice was full of admiration.

'Flambeau, has always been thus and my son's patience and skill with his schooling is undeniable although highly strung, the animal has the courage of a lion.' There was no disguising the pride in Hugh's voice.

The great bay charger reared and plunged as he whirled around. James grasped his lance and without moving in the saddle, brought his brightly caparisoned steed under control; couched his lance, and charged at his opponent. The crowd roared at the clash of steel on steel but it was the young de Audley, who scored the most accurate blow and earned the most points in the first round. With consummate ease, his horse half-reared turned on its haunches and was quickly into his stride. With the next strike, James unseated his adversary to thunderous applause of the crowds. His young brother was dancing up and down in his excitement and their father felt a great swell of pride at his son's victory.

'Well I owe you both a drink, for I wagered a goodly sum on you both winning today.'

'Glad to be of service, Latimer.' Hugh grinned and together they walked down to the ring- side to claim the prize. However, the overall winner of the competition was Gaveston who ultimately scored the most points, much to the delight of the Prince of Wales. The celebrations lasted for a week. By which time the king made ready to head south once again. A number of his senior commanders remained with Edward among their numbers, was Sir Hugh de Audley. Who found himself once more, in the close proximity of the Lady Ankaret. Hugh tried to renew their affair. However, when he learned of the Queen's command to break the relationship, somewhat disgruntled, Hugh was forced to accept the situation. He little realised that Ankaret feared Piers Gaveston far more than she did the Queen for she knew he would besmirch her reputation and any chance of a good marriage would be dashed.

The news of the victory at Stirling reached Isolde some weeks later. She offered up a prayer of thanks after she learned that her husband and sons were safe. However, for Isolde, the period since her men-folk had left for Scotland had been littered with sadness and aggravation. The news of Sir Edmund Mortimer's death had saddened her for she had always thought him an honourable man. By all accounts, he had died of his wounds received at Builth Wells after a skirmish with a Welsh force of rebels. Isolde had also received letters of litigation in connection with her dower from her marriage with Lord Walter Balun.

'This matter was settled, years ago!' Isolde exclaimed as she paced up and down her chamber, the letter clutched in her hand. 'Now that Lord Mortimer is dead, it appears that Walter's nephew, John Balun, is trying to lay claim to the lands at Much Marcle apportioned to me. I declare, if he thinks by bringing this case to court whilst Sir Hugh is absent, he will intimidate me, he will be sorely mistaken.'

Ela smiled, but bent her head so Isolde could not see her expression. Petite Isolde may be, but she had the heart of a lioness, with a temper that could match anyone's, man, woman, or beast.

'If rumours are true, this John Balun, is associated with a gang of trailbastons.'

Isolde stopped her pacing and faced Ela. 'How do you know this?'

'One of the messengers had a near escape with a band of these marauders and Balun was named as one of them. Apparently, he gained a villainous reputation whilst in Gascony and only escaped capture for murder by fleeing to England.'

'Is that so? Well Master John Balun will find that he has no real claim and I shall refer this to the king if need be. We shall see then which one wins the case. A noble widow whose husband and sons serve their country or, this upstart who turns to violence and threats to gain his ends.'

Isolde summoned her scribe and began to dictate letters to her lawyer, her husband and the king.

'I will pay for an armed escort to ensure my letters get through and we shall see who triumphs in court. Once the king is made aware of how the law is abused and sees how his country is plagued by these bands of lawless and murderous felons, I have no doubt; order will be quickly restored and feel sure that he will look on my case with a sympathetic eye.'

'Let us hope so, the Woods, lost all the money for their cattle sales last autumn if you recall, and if not for the community and your generosity, they would have starved and they are not the only family to suffer. Sadly, it is a scourge that affects the whole country.' Ela's words were full of rancour.

Isolde was still in a high state of high dudgeon when her husband and sons eventually returned to Stratton. On taking control once more, Sir Hugh's re-appearance caused a drastic change in the atmosphere as he went about inspecting everything, like a military operation, which upset many, including his wife. Ela knew if it were not for the presence of her sons, Isolde would have taken issue but held back her sharp words for their sake.

However, it was when James stated he wished to visit Heleigh to see his aunt and cousin, before returning to Kennington to join the Prince, that Isolde seized her chance to challenge her husband's high handedness. The two found themselves at loggerheads on many of the issues affecting the running of their estates and their fractious relationship continued until Isolde received a letter summoning her to court for the hearing regarding her widow's dower. In a show of unity, Hugh accompanied his wife to the court and there the couple faced the claimant John Balun.

The court was humming with excitement for by her demeanour, the Lady Isolde de Audley, showed no sense of her inner rage but stood staring directly at her adversary her head held high. The summons was read aloud, and there were heated exchanges between the two lawyers. All the time Isolde remained straight backed, her gaze never left John Balun who began to shuffle his feet but his expression was as belligerent as ever. Eventually when the judge raised his hand for silence, he instructed his clerk to read a letter which bore the heavy seal of the king.

'Today I have heard the arguments for and against this matter and after due consideration

find in favour of ....' A murmur ran round the court; the judge banged his gavel and ordered silence. 'I will continue. I find in favour of Lady de Audley.' This time the court erupted as Balun had brought along a number of his cronies and they now vented their feelings verbally.

Again, the gavel banged down and the judge ordered his officers of the court to eject the noisiest of the opposition. 'I conclude this matter with words from the king so, if anyone here wishes to take this matter to appeal let them understand they will be challenging the will of their sovereign lord, Edward Plantagenet, King of England.'

The court fell silent once more and in his clear, concise voice the judge read out the royal letter so there would be no doubt that the dower rights of the Lady de Audley be upheld and the matter was finally resolved for all time. John Balun's voice echoed round the chamber. 'How can this be a fair judgement when the documents presented by Lady de Audley are forged?' Once more there was an eruption of voices. The judge's gavel banged down again and again in an effort to restore order. Eventually, order was restored. The judge glared at John Balun. 'You will have to satisfy the court of this outrageous claim and until such time as it has been deemed to be otherwise, with evidence to uphold your claim, the judgement stands.'

Sir Hugh's face showed his satisfaction as he moved to embrace his wife. The victory placated the couple and their former hostilities settled, at least for the time being.

§

Meanwhile, James and his younger brother were enjoying their visit to Heleigh. Although it was obvious that Thomas was very frail and therefore could not accompany his cousins and Eve, on their days hunting. He would watch as they departed and returned and listened to their laughter with a profound sense of sadness. He felt his health, caused him to miss so much and blamed his tiredness and fatigue, which never appear to respond to whatever unpleasant potions and pills he was prescribed. He did emerge from his sickbed to join the party for a few hours in the evenings but even that effort took its toll.

One evening after Thomas had retired and young Hugh was playing chess with Lady Katherine, James leaned forward. 'Would you care to take a walk round the gardens with me?'

Eve Clavering looked startled. 'I do not think that would be appropriate do you my lord?'

'I must speak with you before I leave and this seems an opportune moment.' He looked across at his brother and aunt who were obviously enjoying their game and appeared oblivious to their surroundings. Eve hesitated for a moment but eventually rose and the couple left the chamber and walked into the herb garden where the scents of the lavender, sage and thyme, filled the air.

'We cannot linger my lord.' Eve's face was cast in shadows and James could not read her expression.

'You must know how I feel about you. All the while I was in Scotland I thought of you constantly.'

'My lord if you persist in speaking thus I shall have to return to the others. I will not betray Thomas in word or deed.'

'Sometimes we need to speak our hearts however the world and the church would condemn us. It will be enough to know you feel the same.'

Eve moved close to him, and looked up into his face she touched his lips and then placed them on her own. Without further ado, she turned and ran back into the castle leaving James in a plethora of emotions. For now, it was enough to know she loved him but one day, he *would* claim her for his own.

A few days later the two brothers left Heleigh to return to their duties but Hugh noted how quiet his older brother was on their journey south but continued to chatter, even though there was scant response. He mentioned his brother's change of mood to Ela in his usual casual manner little realising the implications of his words.

Ela however, was now convinced that James was emotionally attached to his cousin's intended wife and the thought left her feeling uncomfortable. She could foresee some difficult times ahead that is, if she were proved right. Isolde would be mortified at such a revelation so, Ela decided to keep her fears to herself.

CHAPTER XXI

Early July 1307

The day was hot and humid and the sound of thunder rumbled in the distance. There was a great deal of activity around the tent of the king, who had fainted and fallen from his horse earlier in the day. It was no secret, he was suffering from dysentery subsequently the journey from Carlisle had been painfully slow.

'The king has called for a litter as he wishes to continue the journey on the morrow.'

Sir Aymer de Valance shook his head and stared at the physician.

'And what is your opinion?'

'For what it is worth, the king should not be travelling at all, never mind at the head of an army. His condition is serious but he will not admit it, not even to himself.'

The Earl of Pembroke placed a hand on the man's shoulder. 'We are all in agreement but if Edward Plantagenet has set his mind on a course, there is no man alive who can gainsay his wishes. So I suggest you order the litter and make him as comfortable as possible.'

With a reluctant shrug of his shoulders the physician went to call for the litter to be made ready.

In another part of the camp, Sir Hugh de Audley and his eldest son sat awaiting orders.

'It is blatantly obvious the king will never recover enough to lead this army.' Hugh's words were hushed so that only James could hear.

'After Wallace's brutal execution, no doubt the king thought that he had squashed his main adversary. What followed is still hard to believe. I never thought that the Earl of Carrick would desert and then have himself crowned king of Scotland.'

Hugh scratched his greying russet hair. 'Edward's decision to have Carrick's brothers executed after their capture is one thing, which in my opinion, has only hardened his resolve. With the capture of his wife and sister and then, the Countess of Buchan, whose imprisonment will never bring about the surrender of Brus.'

James sat in silence then hardly above a whisper. 'To seek such vengeance on women is abhorrent to me and goes against all my knightly training. To have the Countess and sister of one's enemy hung in cages on the battlements of Berwick and Roxburgh is' he hesitated, inhumane and ungodly.'

Hugh looked at his son. 'Pray do not voice such sentiments abroad for I fear the actions of Edward Plantagenet in this instance, will undoubtedly unite the Scots against us and Carrick is forged from the same steel as this king. There is no doubt, the murder of the 'Red Comyn' in Dunfermline Abbey, and the king's reaction to the news has hastened his end.'

'Do you really believe Carrick murdered the Earl of Buchan?' James said his voice low and serious.

'Well, as incredible as it may seem, he has been deemed a murderer and excommunicated for an act of sacrilege. Do I personally think it was cold-blooded murder, no! Comyn had a temper and it is more than likely, the two argued and if Comyn pulled a blade on Carrick then ....' his words trailed off.

'What Carrick did next by having himself crowned King of Scotland, was the spark to the current hostilities.'

'Aye, but then the victories of de Valance could have so easily brought the whole conflict to an end but Carrick proved his worth as a commander and gained supporters who may have remained loyal to the English king but for the strategy of fearful retribution. This only appears to have succeeded in sending them into Carrick's camp. Men, who fight for their home and country, have far more fire in their bellies.'

'So, what now?' James's question hung in the air as heavy as the approaching storm.

The look, which passed between them, spoke volumes.

Hugh reached over and patted his son's shoulder.

'Whatever we think will have no relevance, the Prince will be crowned and England will have a new king. Our personal feelings will count for naught. However, we both know the son does not possess the qualities needed to rule England and therefore can only speculate and pray, that the future is not as bleak as we both fear.'

Their discussion came to an end when the voice of their commander rang out summoning the troops to muster in readiness for the day's march. But, the army remained in situ as the king's condition deteriorated. Whispers ran round the camp that the king was dead but there had been no confirmation, only an increase in activity around the king's tent.

No one saw three messengers surreptitiously leave the camp, their mission, to carry letters confirming the death of Edward Plantagenet, in complete secrecy. One hastened to the Queen, the second to the Earl of Lincoln, Henry de Lacy and the third, made his way south to the Prince of Wales, to inform him he was now Edward II of England.

The news eventually reached Stratton by mid August and Isolde and Ela sat for a long time just absorbing the momentous occasion.

'You know, I almost believed, Edward Plantagenet was immortal.' Ela said as she folded her needlework up and put it in her workbasket.

Isolde nodded. 'No doubt there will be great changes, whether for good or ill, only time will reveal. All we can do is hope and pray that this young king will bring an end to the wars.' She paused deep in thought. 'Whatever our personal views on the dead king, we have to acknowledge he was fearlessness, valiant but sometimes cruel and merciless. His ambitions were unswerving and as keen at the end, as they were at the beginning of his reign. One thing I hope, his son has inherited is the gift his father had in his choice in friends and advisors. For certain, the king surrounded himself with men of purpose and good intellect.'

'Amen to that. Although, young Edward's friend the Lord Gaveston may not fit into that mould.' Ela said emphatically.

'Judge him not so harshly. Gaveston is lacking nothing in wit or courage, only discretion and sadly, he has already made powerful enemies. Let us hope that rifts will be healed for the sake of the country's governance.' Isolde's words held a wistful note.

'I thought the young Gascon had been banished from the Prince's....I mean the king's household.'

'I have no doubt that he will have been recalled as soon as Edward learned of his father's death.' The two women exchanged a glance of pure understanding.

'I will begin to make ready your mourning apparel in readiness for the state funeral.' Ela said as she rose stiffly and sighed.

'There is no immediate hurry methinks. It will take a while for the arrangements to be put in place. Besides, we must await the return of my husband.'

At Burgh-on-sands, the main body of troops had remained until the buzz went round; the Prince was expected, any day. This confirmed what most of the men had already surmised their ailing king had died. There was a hushed reverence as many had followed the king on many campaigns and regarded him as a great warrior.

'We'll ne'er see his like again.' The words uttered by a seasoned knight, whose eyes were filled with tears as he spoke. It opened up the floodgate of memories for many of them who sat and recounted the various adventures of victories and defeats in the service of a great king. There was also speculation on what would happen regarding the imminent campaign and wagers were made on the outcome of what the young king's decision would be.

In fact, some of the army proceeded into Scotland whilst the others accompanied the body of the late king on its slow journey south. However, when Carrick and his army failed to show the young Edward led the army back to the Borders and finally on the long road south. There was much speculation on what action regarding Scotland would be taken in the reign of England's new Sovereign.

In early September Sir Hugh de Audley rode into the courtyard of his castle at Stratton. It was obvious from the outset he was deeply troubled. Isolde noted the lines and dark smudges around his eyes, a sure sign of lack of sleep.

'My Lord, you bring with you troublesome times.' Isolde tried to keep her tone as even as possible.

'Aye, indeed. Already there are rumblings of dissent and I fear they will only become louder with time.' He kissed her cheek then looked over at the castle.

'Well whilst you are at home, I suggest you leave such fears outside the walls and enjoy a short respite. Come and see your daughter she has grown apace since your departure.'

'There is precious little time, the king is to lie in a number of holy sites before his burial at Westminster Abbey and I have been commissioned to arrange for the guards.' He snorted. 'More expense.'

'But surely, an honour, my Lord?' Isolde was trying to placate her irate husband.

'Honour, yes but I do not believe the Prince, err King, will be on the same course as his father, in the future.'

'My Lord, pray do not set yourself against our new king at this early stage it must be difficult for him to take command, especially as he must be grieving.'

Hugh de Audley looked at his wife as he handed the reins to his groom.

'I suppose there is merit in what you say nevertheless....' his words melted away as they walked back towards the entrance to the castle.

'I need to have my apparel for the funeral ready before I leave. It will save a journey home to collect them.'

Isolde smiled up at him. 'You will find everything has been dealt with my Lord. All you need do is try everything on so any alterations can be done immediately. You will also find your robes for the Coronation. However, they are not quite finished yet.'

'I commend your efficiency.' He suddenly smiled. 'They need you in the army methinks, you would soon sort out their logistical shortcomings.'

The couple entered into the castle and Isolde felt satisfied she had staved off her husband's uncertain mood. After a few short days, Sir Hugh rode off towards London to prepare for armed men at arms to be in position for when the king's body arrived.

By mid October, Isolde journeyed to the capital for the state funeral. Her heart was heavy for she hated all the pomp and crush of people. She had scant time to meet up with her husband and sons who were escorting the funeral cortège. Thankfully, she had arranged to meet Maudie and the two women sat together in the Abbey.

Through the long Requiem Mass Isolde had time to reflect, on the reign of the late king. Civil wars, his eventual victory over the Welsh and the wars in Scotland were predominant. However, there had also been wars in France and Gascony. He had wrought great changes to the law, with the help of the late Bishop of Bath and Wells, Robert Burnell. The courts of Chancery, which at one time travelled the country with the king now it was permanently sited in London. Edward had fought the landowners over the rights of the Forest Charter and resisted much of the terms laid down in the Magna Carta. The late king had proved a complex character, deeply religious yet, ruthlessly savage against those who opposed him.

Isolde pondered on his successor, as the monks chanted the litany. She mused, the son had inherited little of his father's strength of will and the gossip, already spreading through the court, was of the unhealthy influence the Lord Gaveston was considered to have over the young king. There was no doubt; the decisions of Edward II would affect the lives of every single person who attended the funeral that day. Isolde prayed that her family would continue to prosper. She knew her life would be impacted by the new order but also realised that sometime in the near future, Ela would no longer be at her side and that thought left her feeling bereft. From her early childhood, Ela had remained faithful throughout her early years of tantrums and resentment. Now days, motherhood and marriage had changed many of her own former views and she felt, for the most part, she had control of her emotions. Ela had been right, you could often achieve more by quiet resistance than outright opposition. Whatever the future held she prayed she would find the courage to remain true to herself; to continue as a dutiful wife; to remain healthy to help her children for as long as they needed her.

Finally, she scanned the rows of knights and Earls and saw the bowed head of her husband. His once bright, russet hair now flecked with grey, a sign of the encroaching years. Their relationship during the intervening years, had changed somewhat, she had learned of his strengths and weaknesses but she felt no closer emotionally to him today, than she had done all those years ago when they were first married. There was one fact she had learned that gave her some satisfaction. The Lady Dampierre had been contracted to marry a fellow countryman and therefore would be leaving court in the coming weeks. The strange thing was that Isolde now felt neither, anger or jealousy towards the French woman. It mattered little, for she was and would remain, Lady de Audley no matter how many women her husband bedded.

Love and the grand passion, she had read about but it had never touched her and the only man she had ever felt she could have loved in that way was long dead. However, she did feel she had much to give thanks for and said a sincere prayer to God for the many gifts she had in her life.

The future remained a mystery and the fate of England now lay in the hands of Edward II. The question, was would he prove to be true to his father's ambitions or, had he inherited his grandsire's indecisive characteristics? Only God held the answer. As Isolde left the Abbey after the long service, she made the sign of the cross and stepped out into the milling throng and murmured, 'May God have mercy on us all.'

Maudie turned and smiled. 'The new reign begins!'

THE END

EPILOGUE

The reign of Edward II was a disastrous one. He alienated the ranks of his nobility at the onset by creating Piers Gaveston , the Earl of Cornwall, an earldom previously held by his great uncle, Richard. Edward's failures are well documented and culminated in a rebellion by his cousin, Thomas Plantagenet, Earl of Lancaster In 1322 the rebellion was crushed and, Thomas was executed at Pontefract.

Many of the nobles who had been loyal to Edward I sided with Lancaster which brought about their downfall. Among them was Sir Hugh de Audley, Isolde's husband, who died in 1325/6. Some records say he escaped and died soon after – others that he died in prison.

However, his son and namesake, Hugh the younger, became one of Edward II's favourites along with Roger Damory and William Montacute. During this time Hugh married the widow of Piers Gaveston, Margaret de Clare a wealthy heiress. In 1347, Hugh was created Earl of Gloucester a title previously held by Margaret's brother.

James and Eve Clavering, did live together after the death of her second husband at Bannockburn and the couple had five children. Their eldest son, another James de Audley, became the hero of Poitiers and was created a Knight of the Garter.

[*There is a lively dispute about whether James and Eve were legally married*]. but Douglas Richardson has written, that their marriage did take place but was dissolved two years before James died.

Alice de Audley, Isolde's daughter, married twice' her first husband was Ralph Greystoke[s] and after his death she married Ralph Neville.

So many lives were altered by the personal failings of Edward II which finally resulted in his separation from his wife and his own downfall. A predilection for choosing 'favourites' in positions of power instead of men of ability, proved to be his undoing.

One such 'favourite, Hugh Despencer, [*recently voted the most hated character in history*], was the life- long enemy of the Mortimer family and the nemesis of Roger, Earl of March [d:1330].

Isolde never re-married and died in 1338.

AUTHOR'S NOTE

Isolde de Audley has always been referred to as being a member of the powerful Mortimer family. Frequently argued, that she was Edmund Mortimer's illegitimate daughter, even though there was little evidence to support the claim. Now, Douglas Richardson has discovered old court records which prove Isolde was in fact, the daughter of Sir Roger le Rous [Rus], from Gloucestershire.

The life of Isolde is shrouded in mystery even the date of her birth is uncertain and ranges from 1260 to 1274. What is known is that she married twice once, to Sir Walter Balun around 1285/6 but the marriage was short one due to the death of Walter soon after their marriage.

In 1287, Isolde married for a second time her husband was Hugh de Audley, youngest son of James de Audley, Lord of Heleigh [in Staffordshire], and Ela Longespé. The couple went on to have three surviving children, James, Hugh, who later became the Earl of Gloucester through his marriage to Margaret de Clare, widow of Piers Gaveston and Alice, who married first Ralph Greystoke and later Ralph Neville.

However, Isolde still continues to tantalise us. Why was the land at Arley, purchased in 1276 by Roger Mortimer [d:1282], *as recorded in the Mortimer Cartulary, translated by Barbara Wright*, became part of Isolde's dowry if she was NOT a member of the Mortimer family? However, there was an exchange of land agreed between Walter Balun and Edmund Mortimer, was this a shrewd move by Walter to protect Isolde from his avaricious brother, Reginald after his death?

What we do know for certain, that there was a court case brought by John Balun, nephew of Walter Balun, Isolde's first husband, with regard to her widow's dower of lands and property in Much Marcle. [*The house now known as Hellens is likely to have been part of the claim as the de Audley coat of arms can be seen etched over a gateway*]. The claim, by John Balun that the original documents were fraudulent, was not upheld and Isolde won the case.

This was not the only claim regarding lands held by Isolde as Edmund Mortimer's widow, Margaret Fiennes, also brought a court case against her but she also lost and it was only after Isolde's death in 1338 that Much Marcle and Arley returned to the Mortimer family, as stipulated in the terms of her original dower.

It is fascinating to think that even after 700 years, some mysteries can still be solved and the mountains of medieval documentation that lie in vaults, safes, libraries and museums throughout the world, hold the key to many of the burning questions of the past.

I commend Douglas Richardson for his work in helping to uncover the secrets of England's past, and hope he continues to do so. Even though in this case, it did cause me a few sleepless nights as to whether I should publish Isolde's story but believe the title gives you the clue and no doubt, there were many children whose biological fathers may have been a dark secret – was Isolde one of them?.

Fran Norton

#0063 - 081118 - C0 - 216/140/12 - PB - 9781912419500